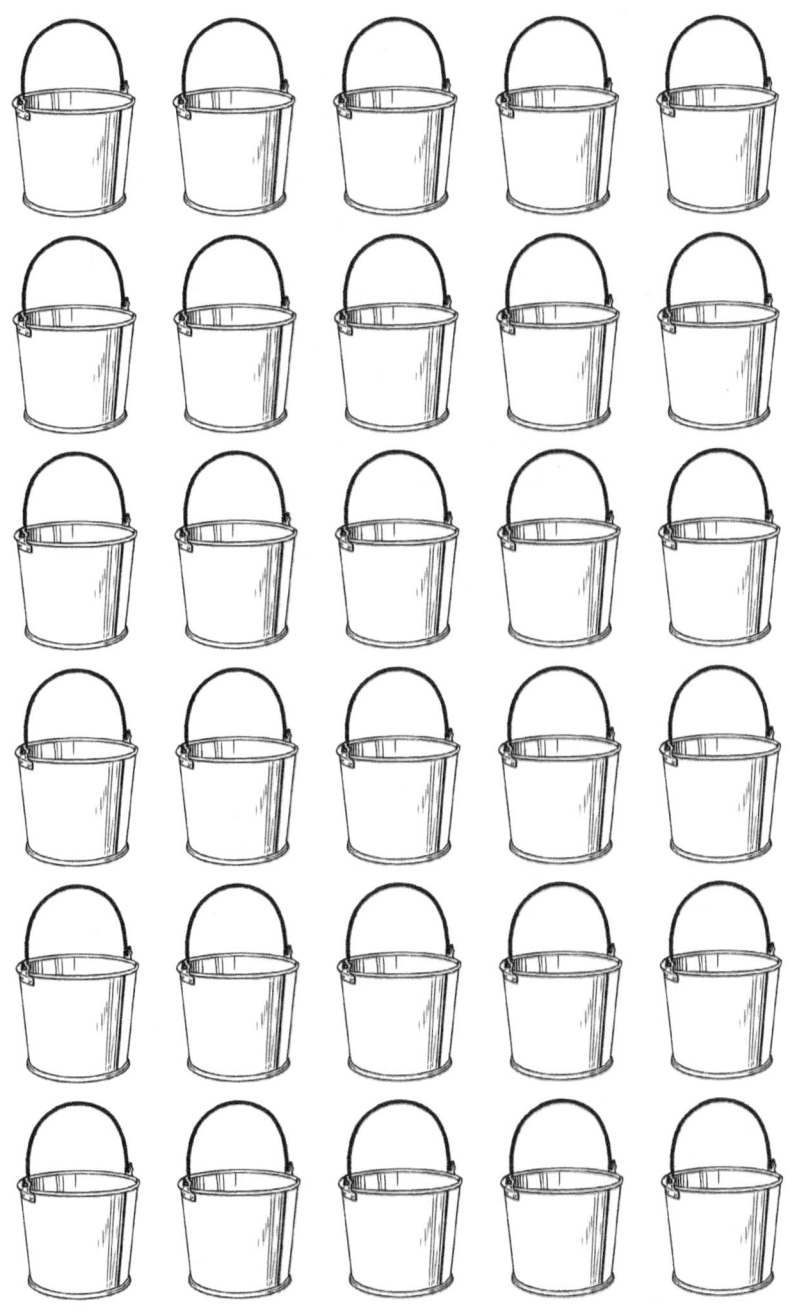

Pure Slush Books

2014

July

Vol. 7

a Pure Slush book

Pure
Slush

2014 July Vol. 7 is edited by Matt Potter and
published by Pure Slush, May 2014.

All stories are copyright © of the individual authors

Cover photograph: European School of Management and Technology,
formerly Deutsche Demokratische Republik Staatsratsgebäude,
Berlin, August 2012
Front cover photograph and design copyright © Matt Potter

ISBN: 978-1-925101-37-9

Find *Pure Slush* at http://pureslush.webs.com

Copies of all *Pure Slush* publications can be bought
at http://pureslush.webs.com/store.htm

All queries re *Pure Slush* can be made
via email to edpureslush@live.com.au

A note on differences in punctuation and spelling

Pure Slush proudly features (both online and in print) writers from all over the English-speaking world. Some speak and write English as their first language, while for others, it's their second or third or even fourth language. Naturally, across all versions of English, there are differences in punctuation and spelling, and even in meaning. These differences are reflected in the stories *Pure Slush* publishes, and it accounts for any differences in punctuation, spelling and meaning found within these pages.

stories by

	James Claffey
Guilie Castillo-Oriard	Gwendolyn Joyce Mintz
Townsend Walker	Stephen V. Ramey
Derek Osborne	Gay Degani
Gloria Garfunkel	Sally-Anne Macomber
John Wentworth Chapin	Mandy Nicol
Lynn Beighley	Margaret Bingel
Andrew Stancek	Darryl Price
Rachel Ambrose	Teresa Burns Gunther
Gill Hoffs	Matt Potter
Susan Tepper	Gary Percesepe
Jessica McHugh	Nathaniel Tower
Shane Simmons	Kimberlee Smith
Michelle Elvy	Vanessa Weibler Paris
Len Kuntz	Joanne Jagoda
Michael Webb	h. l. nelson

Hot Water Guilie Castillo-Oriard   13

La Ronde / Serge and Jimmie Townsend Walker   19

Family Derek Osborne   24

Still Miserable Gloria Garfunkel   31

Maize John Wentworth Chapin   32

Sincerely Lynn Beighley   37

Storm Brewing Andrew Stancek   40

A Woman with a Cat Rachel Ambrose   43

Dildon't Gill Hoffs   46

Tide Susan Tepper   51

Risk and Reward Jessica McHugh   53

Accidents and Emerging Seas Shane Simmons   56

Plastic Michelle Elvy   61

Rave Len Kuntz   67

Seventh Inning Michael Webb   70

From Under His Nose James Claffey   74

The Best Time to Die Gwendolyn Joyce Mintz   78

Birthday Boy Stephen V. Ramey   82

The Trencher Mansion Gay Degani   87

Playing with the Big Boys Sally-Anne Macomber   92

Discipline Mandy Nicol   99

Heat Rises Margaret Bingel   101

All That Trouble Darryl Price   103

Quelle Surprise Teresa Burns Gunther   105

The Mystery of the Manna from Heaven Matt Potter 111

Hazard Gary Percesepe   117

In the Bathroom at Arby's Nathaniel Tower   124

Roadies Kimberlee Smith   128

Family Values Vanessa Weibler Paris   133

The Getaway Joanne Jagoda   136

Hijinks Ensue h. l. nelson   142

Authors   149

Hot Water

by Guilie Castillo-Oriard

Luis Villalobos uses hot water in the shower for the first time since he moved to Curaçao. The tropical rock where opening a car window feels like holding a blow dryer to your face. Where cold showers are as coveted as they're impossible. Even at 2 AM water won't go any cooler than lukewarm.

The mirror is still fogged up when he finishes dressing. Sweatpants, socks, the Timberland fleece he hasn't used since flying back from Mexico in May. His teeth won't stop chattering. And his head. Oh, his head.

Day three of dengue fever. Who knew a mosquito could transmit such misery? He supposes he should be thankful it's not malaria. But dengue comes in varieties. According to Stepan, the legal counsel at Ehrlich and the closest Luis has come to a friend in Curaçao, one of these varieties makes you bleed to death, Ebola-like. Luis's brand-new doctor did say that's not the kind he has. But her assurances sounded mechanical.

Luis doesn't handle illness well. Makes him feel vulnerable. Which he is, isn't everyone, and he understands this in the grooves of his subconscious the way he understands his forehand isn't as good as Nadal's and never will be. But in the heat of the game reality is malleable. Until it's Nadal on the other side of the net. Or, say, a deadly strain of dengue scorching your body.

13

He wants nothing more than to crawl back into bed. But Al has gone over twelve hours without a bathroom break. And without food. He's waiting at the top of the stairs, imploring with big chocolate eyes.

Vulnerability.

"Let's go take a leak, bud."

Al tears down the two flights, nails skidding on wood then on granite tile. When Luis makes it all the way down, nausea blooming like an oil spill under his ribcage, Al is already at the patio doors, wiggling his vast body in spurts, as if impatience is vying with remorse for making such demands on his human.

"Sorry, bud. Should've let you out earlier. Thanks for –"

It takes him a whole new step to realize his foot is wet, another for the why to sink in, and then only because of the smell. "Oh, fuck."

Too late. He's already left a pee-soaked footmark on the rug.

Al cringes, massive shoulders scrunched down to the floor.

"Sshh, it's okay." Luis runs a hand over the dog's trembling head, the silky ears. One has a corner missing. Al came with many scars; most have healed, or disappeared under the regrowth of blue-black fur. Others, like this one, no amount of good food or kind hands can heal. "My fault, man. I know you tried."

The dog dashes out onto the deck as soon as the door opens a crack and around to his favorite palm. Luis leans against the door frame, shivering in the 32-Celsius breeze, and listens to the splash of Al's stream. Sounds like the freaking Nile.

Laughter startles him. No, it's not Al, having suddenly acquired a taste for irony – or the human means of expressing it. Besides, it came from the opposite corner of the deck. But the sound is familiar, pleasingly so. And unsettling. Doesn't belong here.

It belongs to Pélagie Solak.

Must be the fever. He should've stayed in bed, let Al turn the house into a Turkish-market toilet, the kind you roll up your pants to enter and throw away your shoes when you exit.

Al's on the deck, bladder urgencies either satisfied or forgotten, ears perked as high as they go. His face – his whole body – rigid. Listening.

The laughter comes again, from behind the feather hedge of palms separating his yard from Vikram's. Al streaks past him and leaps like a cheetah into the greenery.

"Al!"

But the dog has disappeared. Behind the palms, Vikram shouts something. Metal scrapes on wood. Then Pélagie's voice – it must be her, Al's hearing cannot lie: "Al? Hey, Al! Whatcha doing here?"

Pélagie here. Today. He's not only not at his best but at his worst of worsts. Life has a dirty-bastard sense of humor. At least the palms provide cover. She'll be spared the sight of him quivering like hummingbird wings, turned into this – this wuss. He pushes an arm through the mesh of greenness, far enough, he hopes, that it can be seen from the other side. "Hey, Vikram. Sorry about Al."

"Luis?" His neighbor sounds surprised, but not particularly angry. "Is it the weekend already?"

"No, man. I'm, uh, not feeling well." He catches intermittent glimpses through the palms, mostly of Vikram's pool, just large enough, like his, to escape jacuzzi status. No humans. No Al. "Al, come on, boy. He didn't hurt – uh, anyone, or make a mess, did he?"

"No, no, it's all –"

"We're fine."

It's Pélagie speaking, and her voice sends his flesh into a new eruption of shivers. "Okay. Good. And, uh, hi."

"Hi, Luis."

15

"You know each other?" Vikram sounds understandably bewildered.

"Thanks to this guy," Pélagie says, and Luis imagines her scratching Al's chest, the pure pleasure on the dog's face. "Go on home, Al. Luis, call him."

"Here, boy. Al, come on. Let's go."

Nothing.

"I'll bring him around," Pélagie says.

Luis panics. There's dog pee in his fucking front hall. Will she smell it from the door? What if she wants to come in? But he has no energy to argue. All he seems able to do is call out a strong and determined, "Uh, okay. Thanks."

The front bell rings as he climbs back up on the deck. How the hell did she get here so fast? He throws the rug over Al's puddle – the handwoven cotton is already stained, already doomed. Doorbell rings again. Keys, where are his keys? Kitchen counter? There, on the bookcase. "Coming. Hey, thanks for –"

But it's not Pélagie. It's Milena. His lover. His boss. She's wearing a filmy blouse of big sleeves and big neckline, heels so high and slim he wonders, as he often does, about the miracle of physics that keeps her upright.

"Luigi, I just heard. I would've flown back sooner if I'd known." She pushes past him, sophistication wafting off her, and heads down the hall towards the kitchen. "Did they do a blood test? Dengue's rare this time of year. God, you must be feeling like shit. What's that smell? And where's your monster mongrel? Listen, I had Francelle make you some chicken soup. She's such a good cook. I might take her to Singapore with me, just for the – Luis, close that door already."

But he doesn't. Pélagie's coming down the walk with Al. They both smile when they see Luis, but only Pélagie speaks. "So this is your secret lair, Mr. Hotshot Tax Attorney?"

16

Luis wants to lob back the banter, but his glibness has gone the way of the woolly mammoth. Emotion is building at the base of his throat, and he realizes that what he wants, more than his bed or the snugness of his duvet, more even than to feel well again, what he *needs* is this woman's arms around him. Which is mad, beyond unhinged, not just because he's never felt those arms, has no idea how they'd feel, and how can he need something he's never had, but because Pélagie isn't just out of his league – she's a different sport altogether.

He takes hold of Al's collar. "Thanks for bringing him back."

Pélagie squints at him. "You look – not well. Bad cold?"

"Dengue." There's a certain pride in not being vulnerable to just any common virus. He kind of wishes it was malaria now.

The square of skin between her eyebrows furrows. "How's the fever?"

"Under control." He shrugs.

She comes closer, lifts her hand. Before he can back away or say anything, she's touching his forehead. Cupping his cheek. Small and cool, that hand quiets the tomahawk army that's taken up residence inside him. He leans into it, closes his eyes.

Milena's saying something from the kitchen. She probably found Al's puddle. She'll come looking for Luis, might be starting down the hall right fucking now, towards him, him and Pélagie and this suspended animation. And Milena has the instincts, the sensorial prodigy, of a lioness hunting. The question isn't *will she know*; it's *what will she do*. Luis's career is in her hands. He put it there, seven months ago.

Milena's footsteps are unmistakeable now. Pélagie's hand moves, begins to slide from his cheek. A sort of disappointed relief blows through him. And then, just as the door begins to swing wider, just as Milena's perfume begins to claim the air, Luis crushes Pélagie – so lithe, so scrawny, and yet so vibrantly alive against the arm he slips around her waist – to his chest and plants a lip-mashing, teeth-gnashing, make-the-fifth-grade-class-dork-proud kiss right on her mouth.

Al, with his usual disconnect from the complexities of human endeavor, barks in approval.

2

La Ronde /
Serge and Jimmie

by Townsend Walker

After Serge misreads an email (not an infrequent occurrence) he calls his boyfriend, Jimmie. "Darlink, is Serge."

"Like I wouldn't know your voice."

"Be nice, I be star, show you."

"You? A star?"

"Myron Fopnik new film. I have connection. Know wife. Gloria email this morning."

"Okay, read it to me." Jimmie knows to be patient with Serge and the language.

"Serge my sweet (she call me *my sweet* all time), talked to Myron last night about a role for you. We talked for a long time and read the script carefully. Not now it seems, but maybe later, after the shooting starts roles will become clearer."

"Serge darling, come over, come over now. I need to explain a few things to you about the business."

Like Myron, Jimmie is a film producer, but: shorter track record, more misses than hits, last movie couldn't find a distributor, actors are suing for wages, investor is beyond unhappy. That would be Salvatore Mancuso, aka Sal-your-Pal or Sal-the-Slayer, depending.

Serge jumps into his Miata, drives like he's in no-rules-India to Jimmie's bungalow in Venice Beach, leaps out of the car waving a print-out of the email. Jimmie is waiting by the gate, the middle of his slight pale body tightly wrapped in a strip of blue lycra, a racing Speedo, feet in matching flip flops.

"Hey, not even a kiss for your lover, my big Russian hunk?"

Serge lifts Jimmie above his head and plants a smacker on his belly. "You yummy bear, Jimmie."

By the pool, Jimmie explains Gloria's email. "You see where it says 'not now'? That means never. You see where it says 'maybe'? That means never. You see where it says 'later'? That means never."

"Why she not say that?"

"You have an email with three 'nevers' and they'll buy you a ticket to Newark for a crowd scene? Not going to happen, lover boy. But that's okay, I'll have you to myself. Come here, let Jimmie make everything better."

An hour later. Serge now draped in a zebra stripped robe; Jimmie in a leopard spotted one.

"Want to take a dip before lunch?"

"Serge have appointment."

"Cancel it."

"With Gloria. Maybe they change mind."

"Tell her you'll be late."

Serge frowns. "She my connection."

"Didn't you understand anything I told you about her email? I think you just don't want to stay."

Jimmie sulks off through the sliding door into the living room. Serge panics and runs in after him. "What you do with room?"

"A new friend of mine is getting into the decorating business and using the room to try out ideas. You don't like?"

The incongruity of the aluminum framed glass doors and the 19th Century Victorian interior clash with even Serge's sensibilities, never a strong suit with someone from Vologda. The walls are hung in pool table green velvet dressed with pre-Raphaelite portraits and medieval altar pieces; orange and red oriental carpets overlap on the floor and a tiled faux fireplace has been installed.

"Who this friend decorator?"

"Just a guy I met at Roosterfish. Remember, a couple of weeks ago when you had a late appointment. I got lonely, went down and had a couple of drinks."

"I suspicious, there more to tell Serge."

"You damn Russians never believe anyone. Reason you're here and not there."

"Well, I not tell you what Gloria tell me about other job." Serge plops down pouting in a red velvet covered wing chair.

"Look, there's nothing at all between Phillipe and me. I promise, cross my heart. What's Gloria's other job?"

"Myron tell her about lady in New York City want kill husband because he beat her up."

"So?"

The phone rings next to Jimmie's chair. He's startled someone's calling on his business line. "JBK Productions, James Kilburn speaking." Only a murmur is audible, from the ear piece. Jimmie's face grows paler and tighter, lips compressed to the size of a donut hole.

"Just a minute." He turns to Serge. "Excuse me a minute, can you wait out by the pool while I finish this call, important business."

Ten minutes go by; Jimmie listens, his cheeks become cavernous, his hand shakes. "Sal, look I'll have it for you next week. I promise. Yes, I understand what happens if I don't ... Yeah, Thursday, I promise Sal."

Serge, sent outside, has his nose up to the window, watching. Finally, Jimmie waves him in.

21

"I know, that Frankie. You no want me hear about plans for tonight."

"Listen stupid, that was not Frankie. It was about my last movie. By the way did you ever see it?" Serge shakes his head. "I thought so, even my lover didn't go. Thanks a lot."

Jimmie takes a deep breath, reaches for Serge's hand and leads him to the railed sofa. "Now tell me more about this lady in New York."

"Lady pay to kill husband."

Jimmie leans closer. "How much? A lot?"

"Gloria say Myron say $100,000. Big?"

"Yes, big ... This guy have protection?"

"What mean, protection?"

"Like mob, political, you know, people with guns around him."

"Work for Goldman bank."

Jimmie moves in closer to Serge, put his arm around him, and massages his bicep. "So what's this guy's name?"

"Franklin Lincoln Cabot Three. He called Frank."

"What's he look like?"

"Why you ask questions?"

"You know us movie types, always looking for something interesting to make a film about. More details we get, the better."

"Gloria say sixty three, 250 pounds, pasty like dough face, curly black hair with shiver."

"You mean silver."

"Big nose like bird, shoes with dangle things, Prada Aviators, blue tint. He wear in rain."

Jimmie reaches over, grabs a pen and writes it down. "So I don't forget."

"And he lose kids."

"What do you mean he lose kids?"

"In park, go to big park and lose kids, need police to find."

22

"How did he do that? Oh, never mind."

Jimmie's cell rings. He looks at the number. Swipes to answer. "Not now. I told you later. Yeah, half hour."

"Who that, half hour?"

Jimmie is clearly uncomfortable, his body bobbles, hems and haws, shrugs his shoulders, finally arrives at an answer to disguise Phillipe's call.

"That was one of Phillipe's clients, wants to see his work. Thinking about having him do some rooms for her. She called earlier, I told her I wouldn't be free until two and here she is calling at one, wanting to be here right away and it was just hard to get rid of her, you know how these decorating clients can be. So demanding."

"I wait to see client. Maybe she need personal trainer."

"That's not a good idea."

Serge stands up from the sofa and installs himself in the red wingtip chair facing the door, arms folded, feet spread wide.

"I wait here with you, Jimmie, for Phillipe client."

Thursday

3

July
2014

Family

by Derek Osborne

Eddie's already up and on the 6AM ferry over to Hyannis. He told Anja it's to meet with a local chandler, but he's really meeting a jeweler from Boston, one with a small and rather expensive package. Max has a surprise planned for dinner.

The ring is more than a week overdue so the intimate moment Max had initially planned can't happen. The entire family has come to celebrate The Fourth – both sides – Rebecca thought it was time. The mood onboard is still a bit formal. It's an odd sort of comfort when Joey, Rebecca's younger brother, pulls Max aside and says, "My mom's gonna fuck with you. Do you really have cancer?"

Rebecca's sister, Connie (Consuela, when Mom says it) is there as well. She's nothing like Rebecca, small and shy. Her husband, Jose Ramon, has a forgettable handshake. He's spent the last two days taking the kids into town. There are six from the Perkin's clan and then Rebecca's two nieces. They're a bit confused over who is an uncle, a dad or a grand-dad, but they love camping out in *Gadabout's* salon and Anja has shown them where to buy ice-cream. There have been two closed-door sessions between Rebecca and her mother, one in muted English, the other, much louder, in their native Andalusian. "I do not want to talk about it," Rebecca says when he asks. Max finds it awkward calling a woman his own age 'la senora'.

He's meeting Eddie at Black Eyed Susan's. Jose and Joey are taking the kids for pony rides. As they pull away in the harbor launch it dawns on Max he is leaving the women alone. They're all in the cockpit having coffee. Rebecca is laughing; her mother is tousling Consuela's hair. At some point the launch is closer to town and further from *Gadabout*. They get to the dock and the kids take off. Max looks one more time. *Gadabout* sits quietly at her mooring, a slack line to the ball. The restaurant is just up the street. The Russian girl comes for his order. Eddie arrives a few moments later.

"Brother," he says, even before sitting down, "This guy knows his stuff." He's pulled out the case. The ring is a 5.5ct Oval Blue Sapphire, four pin setting, the band engraved in Elfish. "What does it say?"

"That's for her."

Eddie nods, then pulls out another case. "It's going to be some dinner."

"What the fuck," Max says, a little too loud, drawing some glares from nearby tables.

"You got me thinking," Eddie says. "We haven't had time to talk."

"I know."

"God is coming."

Max reaches across the table and takes Eddie's hand. "Sooner than later, I'm afraid." The last test results weren't good. "You're covered, you know, enough to buy *Gadabout*."

Max lets go of his hand.

"Maybe I and I am home as well," Eddie says, using his native Jamaican, referring to the legend of *Gadabout* having been built to help seven sailors find their way home. A boy at the next table is watching. He leans in to ask his mother a question. Seeing Max, she smiles apologetically.

"Just give me some space in the drawer," Eddie says.

They eat the meal in silence. The Russian girl comes back to ask if they are finished. There won't be a check. Max leaves a ten dollar tip. When they pass by the owner up near the register both men nod; they know one another from the clinic. Outside, it's one of those grand Nantucket days, warm sun and blue sky, painted wood doors, cobblestone street, carved colonial signs. Behind the shop windows are hand stitched leather iPhone cases for $700.00, a pair of sandals for $650.00. By the corner, the haunting eyes of a war-torn girl stare out of the original 3' x 5' McCurry photo – 1.7M.

"Who would write such a check?" Eddie says.

Max looks in through the plate glass window.

"Are we good men?" he asks.

"Yes," Eddie says, without hesitation.

A couple strolls by with two small children, pale, blond, nearly Albino, dressed in matching outfits of khaki and baggy blue cardigan sweaters. They all wear floppy beige hats. The slightest breeze might blow them away.

"Are you asking, are we good enough?" Eddie says.

"I guess."

"We will never be good enough."

He smiles his wonderful smile, laughs and claps Max on the shoulder. "This is why we need wives – to remind us."

Max looks back at the girl in the window.

"Hey," Eddie says, "We have a formal surrender this evening."

"You put it so well."

They also need to go meet with the realtor. It looks like they've found a place onshore.

Back at the boat, Anja greets them by the ladder. "We've had Fourth of July a bit early, I'm afraid."

"How bad," Max says, hoisting up over the rail. It's difficult.

"You couldn't hear them onshore?" Anja motions over her shoulder. "Becky has asked you not disturb her."

"And la senora?"

"In the galley. A good meal solves everything."

"And the others?"

"In the salon playing Parcheesi."

Max looks down the companionway. He can see the women gathered around, the game spread out on the table under the skylight. Connie seems to be fitting right in. Pam looks up and waves him off. The sound of pots and pans can be heard in the galley. He's hit with the smell of paella: lobster, clams, and mussels, fresh tomatoes and spices he does not recognize.

"Anja, could you please get my meds?"

After one OxyContin and two gin and tonics Max is feeling no pain. The kids are back; Jose Ramon fell off. They won't let him live it down. Max is sitting by the helm. The cockpit table is set with extensions to handle the crowd, a white linen table cloth waves in the wind. The kids want their own table down below. Jose and Joey volunteer to chaperone.

"Sorry," Max says, "All hands on deck."

He can hear Rebecca helping her mother. It's an ongoing commentary, sometimes in English, sometimes in Spanish. He's seen her exactly twice. She hands things up the companionway stair and then disappears. There's the hint of a smile, telling him not to worry. She's wearing a light green dress and sleeveless top, her hair is loose and her shoulders freckled. Over the dress is a tattered blue apron; her mother must have brought it. The day is ending, the harbor filled with tall white masts and graceful sheers, the town all gray shingle and lines of white trim, the marshlands crimson and gold. Eddie's brought out a Jadot Pouilly. Candles in glass chimneys, a board with bread, a big bowl of butter. Max calls them all to come up to the cockpit. Even the children get wine.

"To family," he says, "To loved ones here and gone, to this gadabout we call life."

La senora looks at her daughter. Rebecca is looking at Max. Eddie is holding his breath.

"And so," Max says, reaching into his pocket, "in order to bring our two families together ..."

Rebecca catches her breath. "Max, don't."

"I have a proposal."

"Max wait!"

But he's already opened the case. The evening sun catches the sapphire perfectly.

"Shit!" Joey says.

Max is already over the table. He slides off the end and into the hatchway. Anja grabs at the candles. It's a six foot drop. Rebecca is down on her back, she isn't moving.

"Eddie, Mayday!" Max says.

Eddie grabs the mic hanging at the helm. His voice is steady, mechanical. "Mayday Mayday Mayday, this is sailing vessel Gadabout, Gadabout, Gadabout. Nantucket harbor, Nantucket harbor ..."

The response is immediate, a young voice, the hint of an inner-city accent, "All vessels this is US Coast Guard, clear sixteen. Repeat. All vessels clear sixteen. Gadabout, state your emergency."

Max has climbed down, skirting Rebecca's limp body. The kids are all screaming. "Shut up," he yells. He's checking for vitals. Her leg is still hooked in-between the steps. He can't tell if it's broken. He doesn't like the angle of her neck.

"I've got vitals," he yells up on deck.

Eddie is calmly going about it. "Female, early thirties, fell down companionway stair, unconscious, four months pregnant ..." He turns from the mic, looking on shore. "They're manning the boat," he shouts down below. Max can hear the siren in town. "... possible broken leg," Eddie is saying, "possible neck injury ..."

Another voice comes over the radio. "Gadabout, Wind Song II. I'm an OBGYN en route. ETA two minutes. Do not move her! I repeat, do not move her!"

"You hear that?" Eddie shouts down.

Now other docs are checking in, six in all, one of them a neurosurgeon.

"Is that a psychiatrist?" la senora asks. She's more exasperated than anything else. "Sort of," Eddie says.

"Tell him to come, and after he examines those two he can look at me ... for giving my blessing."

There in the cockpit they all stop, trading glances. The Coast Guard boat is at full throttle, its siren up, weaving out through the anchorage, throwing a good-sized wake. The police are blocking off streets. There's a Medevac bus, its lights flashing, the siren loud, then soft, then loud again. The water amplifies everything. The Dock Master, his little work scow with the ring of old tires pushing a fat little wave, is going to reach them first.

"Was that my mother?" Her eyes barely open. "Mama, que dijiste?"

"She's conscious!" Max yells.

"I turned ... I spun so he wouldn't get hurt."

"I know."

Max squeezes her hand, smoothes out her hair, he can feel the swell of the other boats coming alongside. The Dock Master's face appears in the hatchway. Seeing she's awake, he blows out a sigh of relief.

"Yes, Max," she whispers.

"Yes what?"

"Mama dice que esta bien."

29

But then her eyes roll back, there's a tremor. She stops breathing.

"Becca?" Max says, "Becca?"

The Dock Master jumps down the stairs. "Let me in, Max. Move!"

He gently pulls back one of her eyelids. "God damn it!" Then he looks at Max. "We've got to get her flat."

"But they said ..."

"Fuck what they said. C'mon, hold her here and here. Keep her head in that same position ..."

Friday

4

July
2014

Still Miserable

by Gloria Garfunkel

Still miserable Ralph here. These depressions take so damn long to get over. Chloe invites me to a barbecue at a friend's with a pool, but I lie that I have food poisoning and I sleep all day. Haven't seen her much lately as I'm still on a down slide, with that constant lump in my throat like I'm going to cry any second. She's really understanding. I don't know how she puts up with me. I can't put up with me. That's why suicide creeps into my thoughts constantly, though I've sworn myself to abstinence. I hang a flag on my porch to honor our veterans who all have it worse than me and shuffle back to bed and suddenly start crying about their families and fall asleep. At night, Chloe drags me out of bed to watch the fireworks from a hill in town and I can see it is beautiful but find it annoying.

"I wish you were back to your hypomanic self when I met you," she says.

"Me, too. Those were the days. They'll be back and you'll regret you said that."

Saturday

5

July
2014

Maize

by John Wentworth Chapin

Charles starts kicking when he feels the wave engulf his body. The surf rushes past him, through him. He's never certain whether he's caught a wave until the last moment when he finds himself hurtling blindly toward the shore, eyes scrunched tight against the salt. His chest and stomach scrape shells and sand in ankle-deep water as the last of the wave zooms up the beach, smoothing the sand in a blanket of foam. A powerful on-shore current pulls everything forward up the beach. There aren't many other swimmers out today, just a few body-surfers and the occasional wiry old person swimming parallel to the beach beyond the break-line. He has had his eye for a bit on two guys horsing around, laughing and shouting. They have spent plenty of time at the gym, these two, salt water dripping down cuts of lean, tan muscle.

Charles slogs back through the surf to the spot just seaward of the cresting waves. He has to keep from staring at the two guys. It's a heavily gay beach, so a little staring is okay, but creepy is creepy, no matter the flavor of the beach. Charles catches the next wave, a big one, and one of the gym boys rides it with him. They both land spluttering on the sand, laughing, not far from each other. The guy stands and then another wave catches him off-guard and pulls him down. He shouts something to his friend, but Charles pays more attention to the guy's arms, beefy and ringed in matching tribal tattoos.

Tattoo Arms skitters out of the water, escaping the next wave. Charles watches him retreat. The beach is crowded on this long Fourth of July weekend. *Independence Day* – Charles snorts to himself every time he hears it. He doesn't feel very independent. Rehoboth Beach is in Delaware, across state lines; Charles was warned not to leave the state of Maryland.

Fuck that. He didn't commit a crime. *The stupid fuckers in the police department and the mean fuckers in the prosecutor's office can go fucking fuck themselves.* This is what he told Stephanie as he drove east in heavy traffic across the Bay Bridge early yesterday morning.

"You're unhinged, Charles," she said. "Nothing good will come of this."

He was silent, perhaps one of the benefits of *unhinged*, certainly preferable to the kind of unhinged involving screaming and hurling feces at cars from the underpass. He saw a guy do that right next to the city jail. Ever after, when he drove past, he thought about that guy and wondered if the guy was just a lunatic who happened to be tossing shit under the overpass outside the jail, or if the location was somehow central to the story. Was he just out? Was he trying to get back in?

Stephanie continued, "Even if you didn't commit murder, you're committing a real crime now."

Even if you didn't commit murder. Charles didn't much like the way that sounded, so he tapped the 'end-call' button on the steering wheel and Stephanie disappeared. The button icon was red, an old-fashioned phone shape, like a little dumbbell. Phones haven't looked like that in two decades.

Everything's fucked up.

The other gym bunny floats on his back now, just out past where the waves break. He's wearing a square-cut dark yellow Speedo-y suit, trashy and immodest and hot. If Charles had a body like that, he'd wear the same suit.

"How's it going?" Charles says, eyes on the lumpy yellow island.

The guy laughs. "It's going."

Charles gets a good look at him; about 27, lankier than his buddy. "I'm Charles."

"And I'm about as a drunk as I have ever been in the ocean! Woo-hoo!" the guy chortles.

A wave catches them off guard, dousing them. Charles comes up sputtering and laughing. He treads water on the next wave, rubbing the salt from his eyes and spitting, waiting for the guy to come up.

He doesn't come up.

Charles looks around, swimming now, bobbing up to get a glimpse of the guy. He scans the shoreline to spot him walking or swimming toward the beach.

The guy is nowhere to be seen.

What. The. Fuck.

The brown-green water has visibility of only a few inches, so Charles can see nothing when he ducks under. He starts to feel a little panicked, and then he feels something brush against his leg. His first thought is the guy, and Charles dives down again, eyes open in the murky salt water, arms pinwheeling to see if he can find the guy.

Then he thinks – no, realizes – *shark*.

Charles freaks the fuck out.

"SHARK!!!" he yells, waving his arms, and then he just *swims*, panic overtaking him. Every head on the beach turns his direction, people rush to the waterline from the cluster of blankets and umbrellas.

As soon as Charles gets to his feet, he starts running, then turns around backwards in terror as he remembers the guy in the yellow suit. He scans the water for him.

"There is a guy out there – he went under and didn't come up!" Charles gasps, hoping to grab the attention of the nearest beachgoers. People near him shout into the water, trying to get the attention of the few swimmers out there to come ashore.

Tattoo Arms stands at the shoreline, brow scrunched, a beer in each hand.

A crowd forms around Charles and Tattoo Arms, and Charles repeat his story. "He told me he was drunk and then we got surprised by a wave – I mean, what I *think* was a wave – and then he disappeared. I felt something against my leg and –"

The crowd parts and they hear a commotion. Charles follows the gaze of the crowd; a guy leaping now through the waves toward a body tossing in the churning surf. Charles catches a flash of yellow.

Time slows: the crowd grows tighter. Two people begin mouth-to-mouth and chest compressions. There's no movement. No sudden sputtering of salt water and a sigh of relief from the crowd. New volunteers step in to take over the efforts. No sigh of relief from the crowd. After a few minutes of compressions, the guy in the yellow suit stops being a guy and becomes a corpse.

Distant sirens now pierce the air. People are crying or standing mouth agape. There is one very dead body sitting on the beach. Not a drop of blood.

"Did you *see* a shark?" a man asks Charles.

Charles shakes his head, no.

"Why'd you start yelling 'shark' if you didn't see one?" another voice shouts.

There are sharks around here. There most certainly fucking indeed *are* sharks around here – killer sharks. Tiger shark is the only name Charles knows, but he's pretty sure there are lots of varieties.

He was the last person to see this guy alive. This guy who drowned while he was right there, in front of all these people.

Charles hears another voice say, "Hey! Did you drown this guy and then yell shark?"

Only Charles isn't sure if the voice is inside his head or out. He's pretty sure it's inside, but what matters more, what panics Charles as much as the threat of a shark attack, is that he isn't sure.

Sunday

6

July
2014

Sincerely

by Lynn Beighley

Seamus sits across from me, holding my hand on top of the table.

"Jenn," he says, "Thank you for coming. I know you weren't supposed to." He pauses. "I've wanted to be alone with you for a long time." He rubs his thumb across the palm of my hand and I'm getting goosebumps. "I want ..."

"How's your dinner? Can I get you anything?" The perky waitress is back. She's smiling at Seamus. And at the camera that's aimed at us. She's ignoring me, which is refreshingly odd, given the attention I get every time I go out. Maybe she doesn't know who I am.

"Another round?"

"Oh, of course, right away!" There's a word for how she's acting. What is it? Oh, unctuous. She's unctuous. I think she's trying to schmooze Seamus and America.

She glances at me and mouths "bitch." She's not trying to be sneaky. It's exaggerated, so the viewers at home will know that she, like them, hate me. Seamus didn't notice, but Mike, the producer standing behind Seamus did see it, and he's pointing at Miss Perky. I'm supposed to confront her, I guess, but before I can come up with the beginning of an idea about how to react, she's gone. Mike does the shooting himself in the head with a finger gesture.

"You were saying? You want ... ?" I want Seamus to finish that sentence. He wants what? To take me home and make passionate, hot love to me? To get married and have 1.8 kids and a mixed-breed shelter dog? Dessert? What does he want?

"I want … to go to the bathroom," he says, destroying all my plans for either the next 12 hours or 50 years, depending.

I'm alone and the waitress returns. She puts my drink in front of me with enough force to slosh a few drops out of the glass.

"You don't deserve to be happy, Jenn. You're a whore and everyone hates you." She says this while smiling at the camera, so it doesn't have quite the impact she perhaps intended.

"Tell me what you really think. After you bring us a dessert menu," I say. And smile at her. Not a great comeback, but not too bad, considering. Mike shrugs, which I guess is better than suicide by index finger.

Perks huffs and stomps off. Seamus returns and kisses me on the mouth before he sits down. He picks up my hand again.

"Jenn, I want you to listen to me." What? What? Of course I'm listening. But he's not looking at me. He's staring at something behind me.

"I want what's best for you, Jenn. And, well, all those people who voted care about you. They think you should be with Bill." I am flabbergasted. I am gobsmacked. My mouth is open, but I have no words.

"Bill loves you. America knows it. You'd know it too, if you'd give him a chance." Seamus stands. "He's here for you. And you need to be with him."

Seamus is dead to me. Dead.

Mike is grinning like a loon. This was a setup. Well, every time the camera is aimed at me, it's a setup. So I'm not surprised when Seamus turns and walks just out of camera range to stand next to Mike, and yeah, there's Bill, plodding towards me like he does.

What do I do now? If I leave, I'll be hated even more. The show will love it, though, and I'll get more money for all kinds of things. If I stay, the show will love it, because everyone will keep waiting for me to yell or leave. And I'll make more money.

And I've gotten pretty fond of the money. I make money for selling pictures and giving interviews, and I get paid for every second I'm on camera. And now I wonder, what could I do that no one would expect? What could I do that would make me even more money because no one expected it and it would make me even more famous. Or infamous. What should I do?

There is no scenario I can come up with where I won't make more money. That's good, right?

Bill hands me a giant, and I mean GIANT box of Valentine's Day candy. It's July. And it's hot.

"Jenn, I forgive you," Bill says. "You don't need to apologize. Be very careful when you eat these candies, the label says they may contain shell fragments."

What to do? I sip my wine. I open the box. They look okay. I grab four pieces and stuff them all in my mouth.

"OWW, MY TOOF!" I yell, as I pretend to be in great pain. I slip off my chair and writhe around on the floor.

Storm Brewing

by Andrew Stancek

A storm is brewing. Mom is clattering forks and polishing glasses in the kitchen. A pot lid bounces on the floor like a drum but her humming continues uninterrupted. We used to sing that one together, full-voiced, and laugh. *In the Summertime When the Weather is High,* Mungo Jerry. "Life's for living, yeah, that's our philosophy." Been a while since we felt like singing together.

I'm so attuned to temperature, to barometric pressure, to moisture in the air, that I'd be a terrific TV weatherman. I'd just have to work on that bouncy manner, pasted smile and pretense that the temperature in Arizona or rain in Montana is important. This sensitivity to weather is something else I can't take credit for, another side effect of my illness and the concentration on flight, and now it's become second nature.

It's thrilling to hear Mom humming, her mind on something other than Adam, Adam, madamimadam. She must be so tired of me, my gift a curse. Back before the flying, when I was just a sick normal boy, she and Dad would sit together at the kitchen table and play Crazy Eights. She liked to win. Her tongue would wet the corner of her lips when she was about to put down a winning card and she'd laugh hard scooping up the pennies. She's a soprano, but her laugh came from deep within and was throaty, gurgly. She should have had another baby, a normal boy, or even better a little girl she could dress up and teach how to cook and sew. But I guess once I got sick, she and Dad didn't like each other well enough for another child. By then it was over between them. A friend might make her laugh, but she lost track of friends with her devotion to me, too. Maybe we should fly to see her sister. I'll just spread my wings and … A bad joke. I don't have the balance or strength to carry anyone and she wouldn't want to be carried. But she's never dated since Dad left and she should. I wonder if Professor Langeweile is married. He wore no ring and he made me laugh.

This storm is making me uneasy, low pressure and clouds gathering. My joints are sore, like I have growing pains, my eyeballs throb, muscles twitch, everything's out of tune. My nose is filled with the stench of rotting meat.

I wasn't supposed to figure out the flying, I think. It's just not right for humans to fly. In the Old Testament stories Mom read me, when the Israelites worship the golden calf or Assyrian gods, bang! they're hit with the wrath of God. Not a great analogy, I know. I'm not worshipping a damn thing but I still have this foreboding.

When Prometheus brought down fire from Mount Olympus, it could not be taken back, could not be extinguished, and he sure as hell was zapped for his sin. Ever-growing liver, what a nightmare. That's what the Church calls everlasting torment, I guess. Always in pain, always a body part growing, always living with the knowledge it'll get ripped out of you with a sharp beak, no blackouts and no anesthetic, always certain it will never stop, that is hell.

Fire.

Flying.

They're similar. If I'm guilty like Prometheus, then I'll have to suffer like he did. Does. For eternity.

Mom shouldn't be on her own right now. Even more so once I'm punished forever and she's lost me. She's a young woman still. In the movies divorced women date all the time and I'm sure she could find someone nice. When the tabloids were after me, wanting to find out every juicy tidbit, a pretty reporter put her small hand on top of mine and asked about my girlfriends and snorted when I said I didn't have any, that I was busy with birds and research and disease. I think if Mom hadn't been there, she might have offered to be my girlfriend for a night or two, to get a story, a sensational headline. Mom doesn't have Perthes, or a flying gift or a contagious disease, only a wingy son and she shouldn't have to live with pain and be alone.

When I close my eyes I see white lab coats and uniforms, and sometimes I don't even have to close my eyes. That thunder and lightning were so close to each other, it must be a tree in our backyard that was hit. I hope it's not the willow. I hope the birds are okay.

Someone's banging on the door, ignoring the bell, making the house frame shake. *After great pain, a formal feeling comes,* says Dickinson. Mom's not answering the door so I'll go see. I'm chilled, in a stupor. Time for letting go.

A Woman with a Cat

by Rachel Ambrose

"Seriously?" Blake demands of his car, jamming the key deeper into the ignition. The car's engine is making some kind of apologetic whining noise, perhaps as recompense for not starting up like it should. Sorry, boss, I can't today. I feel the need to empathize. I haven't really been the most reliable of employees lately myself, as I've been taking a greater number of sick days than usual, mostly because getting out of bed is harder these days than it really should be. After eliciting another high-pitched groan from the car, Blake turns to me. "I guess we're stuck," he says, running a hand through his thick hair. "You wouldn't happen to have AAA, would you?"

"Of course I don't," I say, feeling bad about it. AAA would be so helpful right now: just pick up a phone and wait for a tow truck. I should have AAA. "But at least it's a beautiful day!" I say, gesturing to the park around us. "And we still have wine from lunch!" We had decided to take the gorgeous July day and go out to the lake, where we brought sandwiches and a very good riesling and chocolates that slowly melted in our hands. But now that we are done and ready to head off to Blake's house for a little afternoon delight, the car won't cooperate.

Blake rolls his eyes at me. "Yeah, great," he says grumpily. "That'll be a good one, the tow truck showing up and both of us sloshed. Fabulous idea, Claire."

I open my mouth and close it again, hurt. "No, I suppose you're right," I manage to squeak past the sudden lump in my throat. "Sorry, just trying to lighten the mood a bit." I try for a laugh, but it comes out strangled and strange, catching in my teeth.

"Well, don't," says Blake. "Say, what do you want to do after this year?"

"Not sure," I reply, not liking where this conversation is going in the least. First he's scolding me, then he's asking me constructive questions about the future. This is going to end horribly, I just know it. "Maybe travel some? I haven't really thought about it."

"No, and I knew that that was going to be your answer," he says, sighing. "You just don't have any ambition, Claire. You're colorless. That's why I have never wanted to paint your portrait, because nothing could be more boring than a beige model in a white background."

I close my eyes and hear myself saying, "not even sepia?" while the blood pounds in my ears, and I knew it, I knew deep down that this was too good to be true, and I want to get out of the car now, before I start crying.

"No, Claire, not even sepia," Blake says, and I grab for the door handle and catapult myself out, the one thing I've done all day that feels like propulsion rather than stasis, and lurch in my pockets for my phone. I stab at the touch screen and listen to the phone ring at the other end, and whisper through trembling lips to my best friend, "Isa? I'm at the lake and I need you to come get me."

Twenty minutes later, after I've secured myself up a tree with the bottle of riesling and have deafened my ears against Blake's half-hearted apologies, Isa pulls up in her tiny car. "Fuck off, you bleeding turd of an asshole," she says calmly to Blake when he asks her for a jump. "Claire, disengage yourself from that tree and that bottle of wine, because I sure as hell am not getting pulled over on an open container violation. Go on, now, put it down and get over here." I toss the bottle in the grass, not caring that a small trickle of wine comes out, slide down the tree and stumble over to Isa's car. She has the radio blasting, and when she asks me where I want to go, I say, "animal shelter" and when she frowns at me, I say, "I want a cat."

More accurately, I want to be the kind of woman who has a cat, who holes up with her cat in her apartment that is artfully messy but altogether hers, well, hers and the cat's. Maybe that's my goal for next year, I think. To be a woman with a cat, to own the cat and the apartment and herself, utterly and completely. But to be a woman with a cat, you have to first acquire a cat. So off to the shelter we zoom, while I drink an entire bottle of Gatorade and make sure I have an ID and a pen, so that I can sign papers for adopting a cat.

An hour after that, we walk into the shelter, which smells strongly of animal and bleach and somehow, also, grease. Walking up to the front desk, I say to the lady standing there tapping on a computer keyboard, "Do you have any cats for adoption? Not kittens, full grown cats, maybe a tom cat," and she looks me up and down, and sniffs, but leads me into a room that is full to bursting with tabby cats, marmalade cats, fat cats and skinny cats. Looking around, I settle on one cat who's looking at me, quizzically, as though asking himself, what is she doing here? and he's huge and fluffy and the color of the pavement after a rain. The lady says his name is Diogenes and that he has been here longer than any of the other cats, and that he's terribly picky about his food, and I say, "that's fine, but so am I, so we'll understand each other."

45

Dildon't

by Gill Hoffs

I was meant to be doubling up with another woman for this client, but then Zhara fell asleep on the grass in the park. Her sunstroke means I'm working alone today.

Usually, I wouldn't mind. Usually, I'm happiest working one-to-one, or one-to-two, or three, or four, but with clients as companions, not my colleagues. It's more difficult to switch to fantasy work mode with someone present who you've borrowed tampons from and swapped whore-stories with.

But I'm not sure about this guy.

His eyes flick about too quickly, his voice pitches from high to low like his balls are dropping instead of swinging damp and hairy below a runty cock as he paces round the hotel room, watching me undress. It doesn't take long, I've only the thinnest of silk blouses on and a pleated black skirt that swishes as I toss it to the floor, and nothing underneath. With most clients I find my nudity empowering, but with this one I just feel vulnerable. He keeps licking his lips, more nervous than he should be for a repeat customer, and the thought of his tongue poking into my mouth or most intimate crevices repels me. I keep my heels on, as detailed in his form back at the office, and brush the tip of my index finger against the grotesque glans of a dildo, lumpen and purple and thick as a toddler's arm.

"Where do you want … me?" I draw out my words and lick my lips back at him, but seductively. I hope.

He pounces and I land awkwardly on the bed with him on top, penis stabbing me, sliming at the top of my thigh, my legs half on half off the mattress. I'm uncomfortable and unable to change position but murmur "Oh baby!" like it's just wonderfully erotic nonetheless. He will *not* be a repeat customer of mine. I'll be sure to tell Zoe to mark him down as a Never Again on my file when I get back to the agency.

"Dirty … bitch …" he mutters between grunts, thrusting at the palm tree I had Akisha trim out of my bush for the summer. I wonder if he knows he's not in yet, or if his runty cock is only used to pushing pudendas rather than pussies.

When he bites me, I scream.

"That's it, you dirty bitch. That's it."

There's nothing coquettish about how I push and struggle now, nothing to suggest I'm enjoying his assault in any way, shape, or form, but he's heavy, solid muscle under a layer of sweaty flab, and when I kick out my high heels connect with nothing at all. And from the way his breathing accelerates, curry fumes hot and unpleasantly moist in my ear, and the thrusting gets wetter against my pubes, I can tell he's enjoying my discomfort, my fear.

Meditations flood my mind as my shoulder pulses "Bite!" "Bite!" "That bastard's bitten you!" "Run away!" and he mutters something about my "tight little arsehole". *You cannot control the actions of others, only how you react.* Dead right. No-one from the agency will be calling me, let alone looking for me, for another hour or so. I am NOT putting up with this shit 'til then.

"Oh baby!" I fake a squeal. "Harder, harder, make me feel it. Give it to this dirty bitch. Give it to me!"

I cheer him on to climax, or try to, anyway, but the bastard slows and lifts his upper body up by pressing down on my upper arms. No eye contact, his type don't usually try to see *you*, just your body and all its possibilities, and I lick my lips and pout and take control of the situation as I lie trapped on the bed.

"Want to see this dirty girl get cleaned up?" I'm thinking a wank-scene in the shower would eat up some of the next hour nicely, and the hot water would soothe my shoulder. But he ignores me and stares at my neck like a farmer checking a chicken for Sunday dinner. Like he's working out how easily his hands would fit around it.

"You want to see me get *really* dirty?" From the twitch of his cock reviving against my thigh I gather it's a yes. "You want to see me fuck that dildo?" Twitch twitch. "I don't know if it can make me feel like you do ... maybe you could help this bad girl ... ?"

And he's off and lying next to me, just like that. I move slowly, slip back into sex-mode, though I'm sure there's blood trickling from my shoulder, and maintain the professionalism that got me into this particular escort agency in the first place. Lick my lips yet again, keep them slightly parted like I can't wait for his cock between them – yeah, right – and ease off the bed. He lies there on the burgundy covers, watching my body as I place my right foot on the bed, careful not to snag the heel on the sheets, and reach my right hand between my legs. I spread myself wide, as if butterflying a shrimp, so he can see the neat pink ridges, and moan when I pinch the fingers of my left hand together on what he probably thinks is my clit.

No twitch.

I lick my fingers.

No twitch.

Pick up the hideous purple dildo from the nearby dresser and circle its tip with my tongue.

Twitch.

Deep throat what I can of it, spreading my fingers wide along its length to make it look like it's further in than it actually is.

Twitch twitch.

Maintain the foot-on-bed-foot-on-floor position and, now the dildo's lubed up with saliva, stick the damn thing in like it's the world's largest Tampax. Both hands on the blunt end, hiding the length, half-shutting my eyes so I can watch him without making him feel too inhibited.

Twitch twitch twitch. Now it looks like a hard-on, only smaller.

I milk the wank for all it's worth, until my client moves on the bed as if preparing to come get me, and then I pull out the dildo with an unappealing (to me but going by his cock, not to him) *slurp*, change positions so I'm now kneeling on the bed with my knees well apart, bring the dildo to my mouth so I can drool plenty of spit on it, and lean forward, weight on one hand, so my arse is high in the air.

"What do you want to go where?" I ask, hoping he doesn't want to toe-fuck me as I can smell his feet over the dewberry-fragranced potpourri in the en suite. I wiggle the dildo a little to tempt him and wonder what Zoe would say to my idea of using the larger dildos as hand-weights if we ever go to a keep-fit class.

And he's at me from behind, thrusting, poking me without lubrication, without even fucking *warning* me. I move my legs, angle my buttocks so they take the brunt of his attentions, his balls swinging against them with every push, and I think "Okay, a bit of ice on my arse tonight and this is bearable" and how there's only maybe another forty minutes or so to go before I can leave but still consider this appointment 'kept' instead of run out on, and then – oh boy – then he uses one hand to pull my hair back hard and reaches with the other for my throat.

This is where our 'date' ends.

I have this one breath left and it's already burning in my chest and throat.

I won't be able to reach his head, his eyes, or anything similarly vulnerable from my current position. Nobody's coming, except, I surmise from his grunts, perhaps him.

I still have the dildo in my hand.

Reaching between my legs I stab awkwardly up and as luck would have it get him *right* in the arsehole *thwack!* He lets go of my hair and throat and squeals, and I feel the warm wet splatter of a satisfied client up my back.

I'm out from under him and grab my clothes from the floor as I strut to the door. I leave his room naked and stride down the corridor in my heels, like I don't give a shit who sees my wounds. And I don't. Then I walk to the lift doors, press the down button, and pull on the expensive top I bought for an ex's wedding and the skirt I know I won't wear again as I wait without turning to check behind me while my escape reaches me from the floor below. When I'm safe, I can cough and cry and swear and be weak.

Nobody comes after me.

My blouse and skirt are sticking to my back and shoulder. They're ruined.

But I'm not.

I add skirt – blouse – ice-pack – plasters to the mental list of things the agency needs to reimburse me for, along with dildo. And start thinking about whether Amsterdam brothels would really be better for me.

Tide

by Susan Tepper

This morning a woman near the oranges tries conversing with him by saying the market keeps the fruit aisle too cold. Pedersen only nods. It seems to give her a signal to go on talking. She isn't bad if women are your thing. When she knocks down an orange from the stack, and a bunch tumble after, he bends to help pick them up. She smiles showing a cracked front tooth; the angle such – that makes a woman look sassy. It won't help, he's thinking, smiling back and moving to the next aisle. Tide. He lifts it by the red handle.

On Fourth of July he'd lit some rockets in the park designated: NO BALL PLAYING, NO FISHING (in the pond), NO ICE-SKATING, NO PICNICS, NO DOGS, NO NUDITY. The sign didn't mention rockets. Pedersen had gone in through the hole he cut in the fence some months earlier; the one blocked by creeper, now, and poison ivy. He wasn't allergic so he didn't cover up.

The first rocket had failed. The second one zinged like a comet leaving its red tail in the black sky. Making him feel alive for the first time in weeks. Weeks since the grammar schools had shut for summer, his little darlings taken away. Shipped off to damp camp grounds and grandparents. Old gnarled hands grabbing them in attic hallways. He knew.

He was about to set off the third rocket, then decided to hold it. Pedersen wasn't sure exactly why.

He carries his Tide swinging it by the red handle – same color the rocket left in the sky. This summer being one long drone aimed at tearing up dusty villages. Places where people talk like they've got food stuck in their windpipes. Pedersen guffaws. The *oranges woman* comes around his other side from the cookie aisle. "It's Kismet," she says grinning.

"Yeah." He squints at the chipped tooth.

She looks down at his Tide. "Industrial strength."

He knows if he takes her home he will hurt her.

Risk and Reward

by Jessica McHugh

Sitting in the sacristy, Edward McKenzie slides his hand over the Lost and Found jar. He's here again. After a month of soldiering through fear, after battling demons that spoke in his mother's slurred voice, he's still here, thinking about the lipstick.

His last class at St. Anthony's ended earlier today, and though most of the other teachers lingered to praise their students' achievements, Father Edward bolted right after the bell, seeking the sanctuary of the sacristy. He survived teaching an eighth grade health studies class, and he wasn't about to push his luck.

Looking into the Lost and Found, the tube of lipstick shines purple amidst pale garbage. He plucks it from castaways, pulls off the lid, and twists the merlot shaft from the tube. He imagines sliding the creamy lipstick across his mouth. Surely a hint of color couldn't hurt, just a quick congratulations on a job well done at St. Anthony's.

His eyes roll upward as the tube nears his lips. "Tell me it's wrong," he whispers. "Give me a sign. Strike me down if you must."

As usual, God offers no reply. But Grandma Eleanor does. Standing in the sun-drenched corner of the room, she's barely visible, but her encouragement is clear enough. At the touch of the merlot lipstick, Edward is drunk on heaven. Waves of delight move through his body as he paints his lips, and though he knows every dip and curve, he looks into a communion plate to verify.

Or boast, he supposes.

You look lovely, dear.

Edward scoffs. "You have to say things like that, Grandma."

Chuckling, she replies. *I certainly don't.*

He gives her a grateful nod, but looking back at his reflection, he sighs, wipes the color off, and tosses the lipstick back into the jar. Slumping down at the desk, he massages his temples and begs the tears not to fall.

A knock on the door straightens Edward's back. He clears his throat, hoping the grief will disappear before he says, "Come in."

Thanks to the summer class, Edward is now used to seeing Nelson Wade in street clothes rather than the surplice he wears as an altar boy, but he's surprised to see him so soon. Entering the sacristy slowly, he gives the priest a small wave.

Edward smiles, but the boy doesn't reciprocate. He leans against the wall, his face somber. "Nelson, what's wrong?" he asks.

"I know, Father Edward."

"You know what?"

He furrows his brow and sighs. "I *know.*"

Grandma Eleanor stands beside Nelson, her hand on his shoulder and eyes fixed on Edward. She nods to her grandson, who sits down, his head bowed.

"I'm sorry, Father Edward," Nelson continues. "I didn't mean to spy – the first time, it was an accident. I saw you with the lipstick and –"

Edward holds up his hand. "You don't have to go on."

"I think I do," he says, stepping forward. "I stood outside this time. I watched you. I watched you put on the lipstick."

Edward turns away, shaking his head. Eleanor appears in front of him, smiling. Why, in the name of all that's holy, is she happy to see her grandson's biggest secret exposed?

"You don't have to admit anything to me, Father," Nelson continues. "You're close enough to God to know what's right."

It's a knife in his heart – painful if Nelson doesn't approve of his lifestyle, and worse if he does. Edward *should* be close enough to know what's right. But what Nelson says next dulls the anguish, like Grandma Eleanor's whisper as she tucked him into bed when he was young.

"I know it's not my place, but you don't seem that happy, Father. Maybe it's because you're not being true to yourself," he says. "You should do what makes you happy."

He looks over his shoulder at the boy. How could a fourteen-year-old so easily articulate what he's spent his entire life trying to grasp?

"I should go, but ..." He gives the priest a small smile. "With all the hearts you touch every week, Father, I figured you deserved to know that feeling, too."

Eleanor leaves with Nelson Wade. She seems to know her grandson craves her advice, but she says nothing. Nelson has already said it all.

The boy's voice resounds in Edward's mind, warming his heart. "Do what makes you happy."

Alone again, Edward reaches into the Lost and Found jar and pockets the lipstick.

Saturday

12

July
2014

Accidents and Emerging Seas

by Shane Simmons

"Hey," I look up to where the voice came from, "anyone sitting here?" An armful of tattoos points to the space beside me. Shaking my head, I toss Sandra's belongings to my other side and the guy sits down. Sat in a dark corner of this function hall, I'd been ordered to wait here while she went off to 'mingle'. Twenty minutes later and still waiting for her return, I go back to fiddling with my phone.

"Don't think I've seen you around, which department do you work in?"

Great, a talker.

"Oh, I don't work at the hospital. I'm just here with someone." Scanning the floor I spot her, standing by the bar with a crowd of shrilling women. I point in her direction. "The one in the red dress, Sandra."

"Mad Sand from A&E?!"

"Mad Sand?"

He laughs, "That's her nickname, *everyone* knows Sandra!"

"That doesn't surprise me in the slightest."

Rapping his fingers on the table, the stranger gives me the impression I'm meant to continue this conversation. I raise my voice above the pounding dance beats.

"Do you work in A&E too?"

"No," he shouts back, "IT, the department everyone forgets about. What do you do?"

If I could bore him enough perhaps he'd move on to someone else.

"I work for the National Trust, digitising their archives for an online library. I spend my day taking photographs of other people's photographs and –"

"Well I thought I'd be designing award-winning games by now, instead I'm telling people to turn their workstations off and back on, all day long!" Swilling the last drop of his pint he sweeps up my empty. "Fancy a top up?"

Whilst he's away, Sandra appears in front of me, eyes swirling under half-closed lids. At her side stands a thin waif in the slimmest, tightest jeans I've ever seen.

"Ahh babes, you're still here ... where I left you ..." she slurs, "This ... is Adam!" She directs her hand up and down his slight frame as if she's introducing the cheap prizes on a game show. "He's sing–" But the IT guy barges past carrying two fresh pints.

"Alright, Sand."

As he sits back down she furrows her brow at him. *"Who – are – you?!"*

He pokes my shoulder, "What did I say, no one knows who we are!" He turns back to Sandra, "It's Callum! We have met before!"

She glares at him, turns and gives me a crooked evil eye before snatching up Adam's hand and yanking him away.

"Well, she *is* called Mad Sand for a reason!" he shouts. "And that stick insect, gayer than a mouthful of cocks!" His right hand slaps down onto my left thigh and he chortles. I squirm around on the sticky plastic leather seat. "Huh."

To my right I notice a mound of jackets and coats which has built up on the edge of the seat, abandoned by those now cavorting the night away. I see Sandra grinding up against the stick insect from earlier, her bra straps glowing pure white under the dance floor spotlights.

"I dunno about you but I'm getting tired of shouting over this lot. I know a cracking bar up the road where the beer doesn't taste like watered down piss!"

As I say it I imagine curling up on the sofa, getting away from the music and all these people I don't know. "Cheers, but I think I'll call it a night. This music's giving me a headache."

"Ah, come on," he looks at his watch, "it's early!"

He strides up the road, "It's only a few minutes from here!"

Inside, the décor looks a bit poncy, low-lights, small groups talking over the murmur of quiet music, a world away from where we've come from.

"You ever tried any of these?" He points to the selection of alien beer bottles.

I poke my neck over the bar. "Tried? There's not one I've heard of."

He grins as he rubs his hands together. "In that case, leave the selecting to me!"

Soon he passes over a bottle, a chalice glass and leads the way to an empty table.

I scan the label, "Delirium Tremens? 8.5%? Pretty strong for a beer, isn't it?"

"Oh, there's far more potent stuff in here!"

All of a sudden the beer bladder strikes. I'll be pissing away the rest of the night.

As I saunter towards the toilets he calls after me, "You had enough yet?"

When I get back there's a different bottle, dripping condensation onto the table.

"Straff ... Hen ... I can't say – Eleven percent?!"

"Yep, this one will really knock your socks off!"

Inside the taxi each speed bump churns my insides. Gassy beer rises in my throat and I taste the sickening bile from my empty stomach. I belch, and wish I'd eaten something earlier on.

I trail him up flights of stairs until we reach the top. Keys jingle in a door.

"Make yourself at home."

I slump on the sofa, but the room swirls of its own accord.

He places a cold bottle in my hand and sits down. "Compared to the last one you had this stuff is virtually water!" His elbow nudges mine.

Picking up the remote, he channel-hops before landing on a station playing heavy rock music and proceeds to nod his head, tap his feet.

"You're Sandra's gay pal, aren't you?"

"Eh?"

"I overheard her the other day, said she was bringing her gay friend to the party. You are the guy she was talking about, aren't you?"

In a sobering moment of clarity, I realise I don't know this guy from jack, but he knows more about me than he should. I'm in his flat which is god knows where and I'm catching up on a game I didn't realise was being played.

I open my eyes wide. Take a deep breath. Squint, try to focus.

"Look, I really should be heading off. I thought that taxi was going to drop me off first ..."

"Aww, come on, at least finish your beer!" His left hand slaps down on my right knee and he takes another swig from his bottle. His hand still on my leg.

Which starts creeping so, so slowly, edging its way upwards.

I'm aware of every stuttered breath I take. I lift the bottle to my lips, take a gulp that sticks in my throat.

I turn to peek at him. He's staring straight at the television screen. Am I so drunk I'm imagining this?

His hand pauses, his fingers stroke the inner reaches of my thigh.

Leaping up, my beer spills down the expensive (for my budget at least) shirt Sandra had picked out for the night.

But he rises calmly. Takes the bottle from my hand and puts it down on the table.

"Best get you out of this, eh?" He smiles. His words, his movements are smooth and cool and undeterred by my abrupt reaction.

"Look ... I –"

He pops open the top button.

I spot the bulge, tenting his jeans.

"Fuck, fuck, fuck ..." I mutter under my breath as his hands close in. He unbuttons the last one and peels open the beery cotton from my skin.

"Come on." He takes my hand, leads me towards the hall.

As we pass the front door, he stops, twists the deadbolt. Flashes me a cheeky smile.

Plastic

by Michelle Elvy

Stevie rides fast. He glides along smooth straightaways and pedals up hills. He's in a hurry, but he's not sure why. She said she'd be there all day – so what's the rush? She said it casually – *come by later*. He really doesn't have to go there *now*. He should wait a while. He should take his time.

His feet pedal faster.

But when he arrives at No. 4 Rock Road and stands in front of the house, sweat dripping down his face and sticking his shirt to his back and chest, he really wishes he had pedalled his Schwinn slower. He's suddenly aware that he smells bad, and that his hair is dirty, and that he is so, so thirsty. He thinks he should ride back home, shower, and come back *later*, like she said – possibly walking. He doesn't even know what to say to her now that he's standing at her door. He runs a hand through his sweaty hair, turns to leave.

But the door opens and the girl standing before him smiles wide and says, "Stevie! I thought you'd never come!"

It's not her. It's Sylvie, her little sister. Relief and disappointment.

The last time he was here was four months back, in March. It was accidental that he came to this house that day, and it was because of Sylvie. He'd come across the small girl wandering up the road looking for her canary, and he'd helped her find it and then bury it in the backyard. He has not seen Sylvie since, so now he's not sure what to say.

"Are you coming in?" Sylvie asks. Her hair is in disarray, one bit flying up distractingly from her left temple, and she's wearing pajamas. Stevie has seen these before – it's the same pair of cat-and-mouse pajamas Sylvie was wearing that day in March.

He smiles. "Do you only ever wear those pajamas?"

"These are my lucky pajamas," she says matter-of-factly. She is tiny, and carries something of a Yoda-like wisdom about her that both intrigues and scares Stevie.

Stevie does not know why she's wearing her lucky pajamas, but before he can ask Sylvie takes his hand and pulls him across the threshold.

"You've come on the right day. I just made lemonade."

She leads him into the kitchen, where there is an assortment of flowers scattered across the table – roses, carnations, tulips, freesia, lillies. They are all yellow.

"These are for Yellow Bird," says Sylvie. "I am re-burying him today."

Stevie suddenly feels queasy. He buried this bird once, all muddy and mangled from bouncing off a car bumper. He does not want to bury it again. He can imagine this small girl – is she five or six, he can't recall – digging up the bones of her bird and burying him all over again, for whatever strange reason. He knows if this is her plan there will be no arguing with her. He does not know Sylvie well, but he understands her will. *She's a force of nature,* Ellie had once said, and on the day he'd helped bury Yellow Bird the first time, Stevie could see why.

But he does not want to bury this bird again. He does not want to bury anyone or anything again. He went last month to Lucky's grave with Manny – on graduation day. They had lain in the large patch of daffodils that surrounded their friend's grave, and they both felt something akin to

62

peace. Finally. But he's not been back to the cemetery since, and he has no intention of playing undertaker or preacher again for this small girl.

Her Yoda eyes look up at him. Stevie wishes he could drink a large glass of lemonade and then just leave. He searches for the right words and opens his mouth to tell Sylvie he can't help her today.

He says, "How can I help?"

He's only ever been to this house twice, and both times he has meant to see Ellie but has instead found himself fully engaged with her six (or is she five?)-year-old sister. And both times it's been because of her lost canary.

"You can help pull all the petals off the flowers," she replies. He looks quizzically at her and she offers an obvious explanation: "Well they won't all fit on a bird's grave, now will they? We're going to scatter the petals over it. Like potpourri."

"Do you put flowers on Yellow Bird's grave a lot?"

"Pretty often."

"Some people use plastic flowers."

"Not me."

"They last forever."

"They're dead. And they don't smell like anything. And nothing lasts forever."

They sit at the table, pulling petals off the flowers and placing them on a large red plate. Sylvie seems content in silence, and Stevie does not feel compelled to talk either, though he wonders where Ellie is. He marvels at the peaceful nature of this small child, how singularly focused she seems to be on the mission at hand. He likes this kind of focus, the clarity of the moment.

"Why today, of all days?"

"Today is the four-month anniversary of Yellow Bird's death," says Sylvie. "I had him four months, then he died. I want his grave to be especially pretty today."

"Seems like a nice idea," says Stevie, but he's wondering whether the girl should just get a cat or a mouse to go with her pajamas. Yellow Bird requires a lot of care, even four months underground.

Just then the kitchen door opens and Ellie walks in. Stevie's glad to see her but then he remembers his sweaty shirt and dirty hair, and he feels clammy all over. To accompany his grime, his palms now exude a sickeningly sweet aroma from the flower petals. He feels Sylvie staring up at him with her taskmaster eyes.

Ellie approaches the table and stands next to Stevie. He hopes the floral aroma will cover his sweaty stench.

"Ready, buttercup?" says Ellie to her sister.

"Yes."

"Let's go then."

Stevie follows the two sisters out the screen door and into the backyard. When they get to the corner where Yellow Bird is buried, Sylvie hands Stevie the plate of flower petals. She goes into the shed and returns with a bag of mulch, which she spreads over what is a very large grave for a very small bird. She then dips her hands into the petals and lets them fall all over the grave. Softly, softly, they cover the ground, and as they fall Stevie feels silly for worrying about something so mundane as body odor. Sylvie is a tiny kid, but he can almost hear her heartbeat, huge and focused solely on loving this small dead thing in the ground. He realizes that Sylvie is the most extraordinary person he's ever met.

Later, sitting on the front porch with Ellie, he admits admiring a six (or is she five?)-year-old. "Your sister's amazing, you know."

"Yeah. I know," is all Ellie says.

He doesn't know what else to say. He doesn't know why he's here, or how he's gotten so entangled with Sylvie and Yellow Bird. It's their story, but somehow he's in it.

He's thinking of the million things he wants to say to Ellie when she breaks the silence.

"You're leaving?"

"Yeah. Florida. How'd you ..."

"Heard through the grapevine."

Silence again. He wishes Sylvie would show up. She'd say the right thing. She'd bring lemonade. Instead it's Ellie who speaks again.

"I just want you to know I think Rick's a complete knob."

"Oh." Woah. He did not see that coming. "Uh, yeah, me, too."

"Sylvie told me you suggested using plastic flowers."

He can't follow the turns in this conversation, if that's what you could really call it. Are they done with Rick already? He'd like to add a few adjectives on the subject of Rick. "Knob" is only the beginning – but it's a good beginning, especially coming from Ellie. "Ummm ..."

"Sylvie and I hate plastic flowers. Our mother used to have them scattered all over the house. So fucking stupid. She even had one of those little vases in her car – with plastic flowers – stuck down with duct tape. Don't know why. It's like no one told her she didn't have to be this stereotype, you know? The chain-smoking alcoholic redneck whose house and car look like she should live in a trailer park? And she uses plastic plates too. When I was little – before I could do any chores like wash dishes – we had plastic plates. Took me a long time to figure out she was too drunk to wash up after a meal, so she used disposable plates and silverware. Can you believe it? Born with a plastic spoon in our mouths."

"That's ... weird."

"So one day, I just got sick of it. Took all the plastic out of the house – spoonsforksknivesflowersplatesvases – and drove it to the dump. Our house is less colourful now. But Sylvie and I eat off our parents' wedding china."

Bitterness seethes through Ellie's chuckle.

"Where'd Sylvie get the flowers for the grave?"

"Martha Stewart's garden, next door." Stevie looks blank so she adds, "It's what we call the neighbor. She's like polar opposite to our mom – perfect garden, perfect house, perfect hair, perfect nails. Her name is Martha. But not Stewart. We just call her that."

Stevie is still trying to follow where this is all going when Ellie takes his hand. "Come inside with me," she says quietly. He thinks they are going back to the kitchen but instead they turn at the hallway and head toward the stairs.

Ellie's quiet footfall leads the way up each wooden stair, her toes showing just a tiny bit of pearly pink polish. Her shorts swish against her inner thighs as they barely touch with each step. A sweet-sour perspiration and fruity shampoo mingle in the air with Stevie's dried sweat. By the time they reach the landing, the hairs on his arms rise up softly and he feels the back of his neck prickle. He licks his lips and wonders if he has bad breath. But none of that matters when Ellie turns and pulls his lips down to hers. They kiss softly in the hallway, and when they finally reach her room and sit on her bed and she pulls his t-shirt up over his head, all he can smell is *her*, every molecule of her breath, her hair, her freckles, her eyelashes, the beads of sweat on her upper lip … He feels a singular focus wash over him for the first time in a long while, a clarity of the moment. He hears a noise downstairs and his mind flits briefly to Sylvie, but then he is back in this moment, where he stays the rest of the afternoon.

In the evening, Ellie and Stevie join Sylvie in the kitchen. She has made dinner. They eat mac and cheese on china plates and drink lemonade from Waterford crystal.

Rave

by Len Kuntz

In Austin, I find myself at a party where everything glows – walls, ceilings, clothes, flesh, tongues, eye balls. I'm not sure if what I'm seeing is real or if the Roofies I took are kicking in. The floors rattle and bounce and keep jumping up, as if they're trying to sit in my lap, even though I'm upright, dancing in the middle of a crowded kitchen, with Rylie, a girl young enough to be the daughter I never had, who's wearing Daisy Dukes and a plaid shirt knotted high above her belly button. The stereo plays country hip-hop, a genre I hadn't known existed. DJ Rusty Crawdad spins music on the kitchen counter where earlier a heap of dirty dishes had been. Now he works the needle, or dials, or some such things with one hand while the other makes lasso motions in the air as a croaky-voiced singer growls, "And I'm a Kid Rock it up and down your block, buy a bottle of scotch and watch lots of crotch."

Rylie does a sloppy stumble into my chest. For a moment I'm afraid she's either passed out, or dead, but then she says, "Isn't this fruckin great," slurring hard before biting my earlobe.

I met Rylie at Starbucks where she was working, where she remade my double-mocha-ginger-spice-no-foam-chia-tea-latte three times without ever getting it right. Rylie was worried I'd complain to her boss, and as a favor, she invited me to this country-themed "Rave."

I hadn't thought I'd come, but once I did, I hadn't thought Rylie would give me the time of the day, though upon seeing me, Rylie pressed her huge breasts against me and squealed. "I'm so glad you showed. You're, like, the hottest old guy I know." To wit, I thought: I hadn't realized we knew each other. I hadn't thought forty-two was all that old.

Rylie has a lot of friends who are just as gorgeous and as daft as she is. When not dancing, they huddle together, bobbing like skiffs, nodding quite a bit and tittering before any sentence is finished, even if someone's just remarking on the weather. One of them – Tessa – rubs the back of my thigh and squeezes my buttocks anytime I get near. She has diamond piercings over each eyebrow that glitter like bright, white halos. Earlier, as I was refilling my radioactive-looking cocktail, Tessa leaned in and whispered, "I bet you really know how to clean a girl's carpet."

The house we're in is a monster, containing millions of rooms and crawl spaces with their doors flung open, revealing couples engaged in all kinds of salacious acts, the participants oblivious to anyone or anything. Rylie explains it's the Sigma Chi fraternity, that their charter was revoked after a hazing incident involving a pledge and a goat in heat, and that the house has remained vacant since, except when people want to rent it for engagements such as this.

All night long Rylie hovers around me, clinging when she can, fawning and groping. Towards midnight, we end up in a room where someone's pinned a gigantic Confederate flag across one wall, with a twelve foot-long aquarium stationed on the other wall opposite it.

Rylie grabs my shirt placket and pulls me onto the bed. Her pupils are brown quarters, her mouth a trapdoor sprung open.

When she says, "It's now or never, Pappa," my stomach clutches, and I don't know if it's because of what she's inferring, or what she's called me.

The aquarium makes a steady gurgling noise that gets me dizzy. Bright, fluorescent fish flip through the gleaming clear water, leaving a trail of air bubbles in their wake.

"Kiss me like you mean it," Rylie says, tugging on my beard stubble. "Then fuck me like you don't."

I'm tempted, of course, but I push her away instead.

Rylie grabs fistfuls of my hair and yanks and yanks, shrieking like a cat with its tail caught in the garbage disposal. I think she's having an epileptic attack, or some such thing, so I pull her inside my chest, which is slick with Rave-induced sweat, and hold her there, as if trying to calm a frightened pet.

I say, "It's okay."

I say, "Everything's all right."

She asks me again to do things to her. She says she'll call me Daddy. She says that's what all the boys like.

I cup Rylie's hands. Over her head, in the tank, a rainbow-striped fish hovers by the glass, as if listening and watching.

"What happened?" I ask. "You can tell me. Go ahead. What happened to you when you were little?"

Seventh Inning

by Michael Webb

I wait for her to come to bed. It is the All Star Break, otherwise known as Christmas in July for the lonely / horny major leaguers who aren't selected for the Midsummer Classic. I try to minimize the distraction I cause, but it's always an issue, a week without me interrupted by sudden Daddy overload. Even if the team is home, I'm constantly leaving before they go to bed, missing activities, missing out, becoming an absentee father, absentee husband, just the guy who brings home the money that pays for the lessons and the shoes, the manicures and the brand name handbags.

She comes in, finally having addressed the last of the requests for water and stories and reassurances that permission slips were signed for the camp trip to the zoo tomorrow. I watch her prepare for bed, the television on silently behind her back as she brushes her hair out at her makeup table. I watch the way her Arizona State t-shirt flexes and moves with her body. She is still the woman I married, but somehow more refined. Children have made her more serious, thicker, more grounded. Someone to take seriously. She is as beautiful as she ever was. And she mentioned thinking about a third child, and my pulse thrummed excitedly at the prospect of trying to make that happen. Perhaps tonight.

"Lucasita called me this morning," she says.

"Oh?" I say, not knowing what to add.

"Yes, I guess she sees me as a mentor. Or something. All this is new to her. Being a mom, being a ballplayer's wife. All of it."

"I suppose it must be," I say evenly. Her voice is too bright for the conversation, like she is trying too hard to sound casual.

"She asked me if you were out last night," she says. She knows I wasn't. Yesterday, the first day of the All Star break I spent with her, going on the camp run, shopping for groceries, then odds and ends at Target before a spinach salad for lunch and the reverse trip in the afternoon. I probably wasn't more than a hundred feet from her the entire day. I feel a trap coming, like a high school boy trying to explain who will be supervising the party.

"You told her I was with you."

"Of course I did. And then she told me about the conversation you had with her in May. In the park. Do you remember?"

I picture Lucasita, Juan's wife, her tiny swollen feet barely touching the pedals of their gigantic car as they inched their way out of the player's parking area.

"I think so," I say carefully.

"She said you mentioned being out with him. The night before. You never told me you've been out with Juan."

"I haven't," I say softly.

"Why did you lie to her, Mark?"

"To support Juan," I say. On the TV, a computer-animated lizard is trying to sell me insurance. I swallow hard, suddenly needing a glass of water. Or a beer.

"What does that mean?"

"Juan's a teammate," I say, hating how lame it feels even as I hear the words coming out. "We support each other. We're brothers. I cover for him, because he saves my ass in the field. Saves runs, which lowers my ERA, which raises my asking price, which makes the money that pays for our beautiful house," I say, standing up and moving towards the bathroom. "The money that pays for all those Manolo Blahniks you love so much," I say a little too loudly.

"That's not fair, Mark," she says, tugging at the tangles at the end of her hair. "And you know it. I could have gone to law school. I had the grades. I could have paid for my own goddamned shoes. If it's that fucking important to you, I'll sell the damn things on eBay. Are we that fucking broke?"

I pour myself the water, gulping it down in several long swallows, then sucking in a deep breath. She is staring daggers at me, her arms folded tight on her chest, the hairbrush flung aside, forgotten. "I'm sorry. It's not the shoes," I say. "I'm sorry I lied. I shouldn't have. I know."

"Say that to Lucasita," she spits bitterly.

"I know," I say quickly, my arms thrown wide as I stand against the bathroom door. "But I have to have Juan on my side. You have to understand, I can't sell him out. I can't sell him out because I need him to make plays for me. And I can't sell him out because I can't get a rep as a guy who does that!" My hands fall as I realize she isn't getting it. Or isn't buying it.

"A rep?" she says with exasperation. "A rep? What are you, a bunch of 12-year olds?"

"Essentially," I say. I think about Sam Madden, who I played with in New York, who could hit and field but was suddenly unemployable with one truthful interview too many.

"Listen, Mark," she says, standing up straight. I stare at her legs, bare and trim and perfect. "For however long we are here, Lucasita is my friend. You and Juan and you overgrown children can play your bullshit games with someone else. You don't lie to me, and you don't lie to my friend. Period. You know, Mark? That's going to be your daughter someday. Do you want some 22-year old shortstop lying to your pregnant daughter while he's out at a strip club?" I watch her pick her brush up and put it back on her makeup table, her motions fluid and precise like a dancer. I marvel at her beauty, two kids and still pretty as a schoolgirl.

She turns out the light, slipping under the covers and defiantly facing away from me. I stare at the TV screen, a busty fan flirting silently with a catcher in a shampoo commercial, the flashes of light playing across the Egyptian cotton sheets that cover her body, only a splash of hair emerging from the top.

"I swear," she says slowly. "I don't know why the fuck we put up with you."

"Ballplayers?" I say.

"Men," she says to the wall.

I consider getting up to go downstairs, but just continue to sit there, watching the All Star Game play out silently on the screen. Eventually, I think, someone will win.

From Under
His Nose

by James Claffey

The post brings a letter from the solicitors. The Bird sups the cup of tea as he reads the typewritten page, and when he gleans the message it contains, splutters the tarry brew all over the kitchen table. "By Jesus, I'll not let those bitches take the roof over my head." He slams the teacup on the table and makes a beeline for the O'Meara & McCarthy, Solicitors at Law, over on Casement Place.

Mary Igoe, with the lazy eye, perches on the desk, legs crossed, the *Irish Press* open and the radio playing the Gay Byrne Hour. The Bird's entrance sends her scurrying for the safety of behind the desk.

"How are you, Mr. Mahony?" she asks.

"Don't Mister Mahony me," he says, distracted by the one eye on the door and the other on his movements. "I want to see one of the chiefs."

"Oh, they're in conference," she says. "I can take a message and make an appointment for you."

"Appointment? For to have them steal the house from under my arse? Scutter them. Go and tell them I'm here and I'm not leaving until I see one of them." He sits in the old armchair by the window and grips the armrests as if an earthquake were about to rattle the crockery in the kitchen presses.

"I said," she says, "Conference. No appointment for you, so you'll have to make one and come back."

"Back? Back, while they're selling my home to the fucking nuns up the road?" His roaring echoes off the walls of the small office and a door opens and the bald, red-faced O'Meara of the practice emerges to see what the commotion might be.

"Oh. Mahony. Listen, if it's about the nuns and the old homestead, you've not a leg to stand on."

"You'd better explain something to me, and fast. I'll bloody open your skull if you don't," the Bird says.

"Come through, for Christ's sake. Come through, now."

The two men leave Mary Igoe one-eying the obituaries in the paper for new opportunities for the firm, and in the back office the Bird sits on the offered chair.

"Listen, your father was in debt. Sure the business was going downhill these past twenty years. He did a deal with the ladies in the convent and you're all right in the house as long as you like, but when you depart this world, the title passes to them, along with all that's in it."

The Bird scratches behind his ear. He's unsure at what he's been told. "Do you mean I can live there, but the nuns will own it when I die?"

"That's the long and the short of it, Bird." O'Meara shakes his head, holds both hands up in supplication, and says, "We're only carrying out your father's wishes, you understand."

"Why wasn't I told of it before this?"

"Aren't we only having the reading of the will this month," O'Meara says, smiling. "You'll hear it all again there."

"Bugger those old hens. They'll murder me in my bed to get the place sooner," the Bird says, standing up and making for the door. "Curse the pair of you in this bloody business," he shouts, as he departs without a backward glance at Mary Igoe, who's already spreading the news through the parish grapevine on the party phone line.

§

In the cubby where the mother kept the bread, he finds the stowed bottles and opens the first one to hand. Blue lights cracking black sky, the Bird holds his head to stop the buzzing from driving him mad. Ever since the day's post arrived with the news, ever since he discovered the nuns were on the deed and the parents had turned the house over to the bitches, he's emptied the bottle of Tullamore Dew, and is now halfway down the Smirnoff. "Vicious harpies," he says, the words a slurry of drink and venom. "And the business, too. Hearses, coffins, brass and silver fittings, all turned over to the Holy Roman Empire."

"I have my bicycle," he says, falling against the range in the kitchen. "I'll head off and find that French one, and sure we'll marry and that'll be the saving of me." More blue and black and on the way to the floor the Bird's head connects with the edge of the kitchen table and he opens a long gash that pours red on the linoleum. He sleeps fitful drunk through the midday church bells ringing out the Angelus, and some time after the rain hammers the windowpanes he groggily climbs to his feet and makes his way to the bathroom where he doses his head with mercurochrome and cotton wool.

Shock, and the specter of being swindled of his birthright combine to torment the Bird as he gathers the evidence of his morning's debauchery. He slings the empties in the dustbin outside the back door, the house number painted in white on the silver aluminum. He's a good mind to roll the dustbin down the road and fling it through the window of the convent, but he'll only end up in the barracks without any means to bail himself out. Across the road, two leather-jacketed punks creep along the path, their perfect Mohawks sharp-shadowed against the backdrop of concrete as they pass the police station.

Stutter-stepping down the path with his bicycle, the Bird is an underdog in the game of love. His ears tipped red by the brisk breeze, he sails off towards Hogan's in Clara, the rear mudguard rattling away as he maneuvers the potholes. At the corner of Main Street, McCarthy, the other solicitor, drives by in his brown Mercedes, the morning cigar dangling from his lips. The Bird haughs up a mouthful of phlegm and spits it at the passing car. "Cur," he says, and pedals away triumphant.

Still woozy from his overindulgence, he wobbles from side to side, puddles splashing his pants leg as he passes through the dirty rainwater. Off to the east the clouds darken, large, rolling cumulus, their promise of more rain nearing as they tumble towards the town. He knows the drink is behind his hopeless fantasy about Melodie and the possibility of her even being in Ireland. As his father used to say, "God loves a trier," and the Bird smiles to himself, the faint sound of his father's voice echoing in the street.

The Best Time
to Die

by Gwendolyn Joyce Mintz

Diane, who's been waiting, lifts her hand and waves when Aaron, with Phil in the passenger seat, drives up. She's sitting on the wooden FOR SALE sign staked in the lawn.

"I'd buy that," Phil says under his breath.

Aaron lets out a loud chuckle. "It's a shame you aren't taken with Diane," he says.

Phil's face colors. "I didn't mean to say that out loud. But since I've already said too much, I might as well add that she has no idea of what she brings to the world."

Nodding, Aaron lifts the handle, pushes open the door. He steps out. "That she does not. And that's what makes Mora crazy."

He shuts the door and greets Diane.

She stands and meets him in front of the car.

They chat. Then Diane heads toward the front door. Aaron raps his knuckles on the hood, gestures for Phil to join.

Phil opens the door, pulls himself out, heads, too, for the building.

It's just the three of them tonight. Mora had to work but Aaron had confessed (when he called the other two to invite them to his place) that he'd been prepared to ask her not to come.

"Your place looks different in the daytime," Diane says. "Bigger."

Aaron is twisting the key in the lock. "I only live on the bottom. My grandparents converted their house into two apartments when they moved," he continues as he opens the door. "They left it to me when they died." He gestures Diane and Phil in. "I lived with my dad's parents for a lot of my life. My parents were crazy; my grandparents, not so much."

His friends laugh.

There is no furniture in the living room except for a recliner pushed sideways against one wall. A green-plaid blanket is folded on the seat, a pillow atop it. Against the adjacent wall is a card table holding a lamp, a few books, a cup of pens and a stack of paper.

"I hope this is not your regular bachelor pad," Diane says. "Let me guess," she tells Aaron as she poses by the recliner like a game show model. "Daytime." She presses the lever and the chair falls back, leg rest up. "Nighttime."

"Exactly," Aaron replies.

She walks over to the kitchen area and peers in. "Your lap holds your meals?"

"Something like that," Aaron replies as he steps into the kitchen. "What I do still have is beer and wine. Any takers?"

They sit on the floor. Aaron, back against a wall, legs stretched before him, crossed at the ankle. Arms folded across his chest, he holds a bottled beer in one hand.

Phil leans against the recliner and Diane sits crossed-legged by the door. Both sip at plastic cups of Chardonnay.

"I can't believe it's July already," Diane says.

"I didn't think I'd still be here," Phil adds.

Aaron grunts. "You should be dead by now, huh?"

Diane tells Aaron that "just yesterday" they were forming this "Suicide Club."

"So what happens if a new year rolls around and you're still here?" she asks him.

Aaron shakes his head. He points the bottle at a piece of paper taped to the wall above her. "Every day I cross something off is another day closer."

Curious, Diane stands and reads part of the list:

Buy motorcycle – ride it to Tucson
Pay overdue library fines
Spend Valentine's Day with Mora
~~Call Aunt Lily~~
~~Give away/sell furniture~~
~~Pare clothing to 2 weeks – get rid of rest~~
~~Shred documents~~
Sell house
Have utilities disconnected

"Well, you *will* be here next year if you have to get all of this done," her finger points toward the one caveat.

Aaron rises, reads it and scratches the side of his head. "Don't have an answer for that." He returns to his place on the floor.

"How 'bout you Phil," Diane says, returning to the hardwood as well. "You have a date in mind?"

He shakes his head in slow motion. "Still working on the best time to die." He sighs. "Either of you feeling guilty?"

Diane shakes her head. "Not a bit. Not to sound mean but the people left behind cannot possibly hurt as much as the person gone."

Phil contradicts her. "I think everyone involved hurts."

"Is it so bad for you, Phil?"

He looks Diane full in the face. "My parents used to tell me that I could have what others have, but that's not true. People aren't big enough to look past the way others look."

"Amen." Diane interjects. "It goes both ways though."

"Yeah, well, I'm tired of being looked at like I'm the modern-day Quasimodo."

"Maybe you just need to ask someone out," Aaron suggests.

"I did. She said 'no'."

"Who?" Aaron takes his place back on the floor.

"Lindsey."

"Our server?" Diane asks.

"Yeah."

Aaron releases a breath. "I'm sorry, Man."

Phil shakes the apology away. "If I had to choose between you and me, I'd choose you too."

The laughter that follows is awkward but feels good.

"Maybe I've ignored just how much I'm hurting." He lifts the cup to his mouth and empties it. Setting it aside, he says, "I'm blabbering, aren't I?"

"Alcohol always loosens the tongue," Aaron comments.

Phil chuckles as he shakes his head. "I'm glad it's just us. I like Mora, but –"

"We all do, some more than others." Diane turns her attention from Phil.

"Ouch," Aaron says.

"We're being honest here," she responds.

He nods. "You're right. Objection overruled."

Birthday Boy

by Stephen V. Ramey

It's my birthday. Fifty-eight glorious years. I roll onto my back. Plastic tarp crinkles. My bones ache. Light smears through the glass block window.

"Crap." I overslept. While the cops don't often check these basements, they sometimes do on their morning rounds. If I'm caught, I go to jail. I got my warning last week. I'm in the system now, albeit under an alias. They just assumed I wouldn't have ID. Now, I'm a notarized street bum. Be on the lookout. Disarmed and odiferous.

I won't pretend to have suffered the way truly homeless people do. I have some cash, an ATM card, keys to many things should I choose to use them. I bought a tarp the first day, having read on a blog that that's what to do when you're homeless. A backpack too. I'm actually pretty proud of how I've handled my walkabout; that's how I prefer to think of this foray onto the skin of New Castle's underbelly. Research for the novel, a stroll through my character's inner terrain.

Rose's voice pops into my head: *Oh, it's more than that.* Of course she's wrong. Just because Rose is pagan, does not make her wise.

I need to release the past if I am to find my path forward. It's been a month since Amanda's ghost shocked my senses clean. Cancer is a natural process. I don't want to live out my life as an invalid, don't want to be a burden for the people I care about, or rack up reams of debt. That's my truth. That's what I should cling to when I find myself peeing in an alley.

Which reminds me.

After relieving myself against the far wall – a process like squeezing glue from a bottle with a clogged nozzle – I wad the tarp into the backpack, ease open the door, and squint up a half-flight of steps to the street. *All clear.*

Outside, I reposition the padlock so the door looks intact. I can squat here for weeks if I play my cards right.

I pull the backpack tight between my shoulders and climb the steps, looking as if I belong. That was probably the most difficult adjustment. When you're newly homeless it feels like everyone is watching for an excuse to call the cops or beat you down. After a week or so, you realize you're invisible.

Most of the homeless are solitary by day. We disperse, scavenge, nap on benches by the library. When we do pass, it's like jungle cats. Our hackles rise, and we're ready to defend our territory even if we have nothing to defend.

At night, there's more community, small groups, barrel fires when the opportunity presents. Alcohol and drugs, but mostly companionship. We're wary, though, and when we bed down, we do so with one eye open.

I turn onto Mill. There's a seventies-style shopping plaza across the street. It hasn't been fully occupied since Anne and I moved to New Castle. I try to imagine shoppers, kids laughing, shops filled with consumer goods. Longtime residents tell us that's how it used to be. In moments like this, I understand their nostalgia. It's easier to look back than forward when you are dying.

The dumpster behind The Confluence has been picked clean, but I find an intact fast food bag in one of the trash cans. As I cross the bridge to East Side I toss cold fries to the fish and down a pair of chicken nuggets. Tent City is out of sight around the river's bend. *Come back when you are ready*, I recall the tent woman saying. I'm not ready yet.

A crowd has gathered at the day-old bread shop. Usually they roll out a shopping cart filled with stale product by 10 AM, but I'm not in the mood to fight over dry loaves. I continue past the shop. If you keep moving, the cops are unlikely to hassle you, and business owners don't get cranky.

A savory smell penetrates the cold-air sterility, a hint of lamb charring. I think of the three twenties tucked into my sock. *Four Brothers Bistro* is across the street. I can splurge.

One look at my dirt-stained jeans, the frayed hem of my shirt tells me otherwise. *Keep moving like a shark*, I think, only I don't feel like a predator, but a minnow.

I head back toward town. A bank sign flashes: *July 18, 84°, 11:38.* "Happy birthday, Stephen." I slide my wallet out – keep it in a side pocket, not the rear – and open it. Anne smiles from behind a plastic shield. I emailed her from the library the day after Amanda's ghost. *Gone fishing*, I typed. *You know that I love you, but it's come to that.*

I told her once that I had made a pact with my suicidal teenage self, that if things ever got unbearable I would just take off, go fishing, and sort it out in solitude. Having endured her own bouts with depression, Anne said she understood. I haven't seen signs of a search effort, so maybe she did.

"Hey S-Man!" A scrawny guy with a guitar slung over his shoulder hurries across the library lawn. Dave is a Desert Storm vet who's been homeless for a few years. As a street corner evangelist and talented vocalist, he does pretty well for himself. It's his temper, sudden like a storm, that gets him into trouble.

He meets me at the corner. His smile is missing no teeth; his eyes are polished stones inset into a hardened face.

"It's a glorious day, S-Man," he says. "Did you sleep last night? I didn't see you at the shelter." Dave tells me often that I should check into the Men's Shelter across the river from the Riverplex. Free meals, beds, hot showers. You have to get there early, of course, but they're good folks. I did stay a couple nights, but the required prayer and rigid scheduling turned me off. Plus, it would be one of the first places Anne might look.

We cross the street together. Gentle twangs sound from the guitar as Dave walks. A sweet smell wafts from the Cake Eater Bakery. My hunger erupts. I dredge my pocket for coins garnered from sidewalk scavenging.

"Don't waste your resources," Dave says. "The Presby is doing a prayer breakfast today. They probably have something left."

I stop. "It's my birthday." Coins press into my fist like the nodules in my prostate. I haven't told anyone about the cancer. That's part of a code I'm learning. We don't complain about problems we all have. You don't become homeless by accident.

"How much you got?" Dave says.

I count. "Dollar-forty-five."

He gives my shoulder a squeeze. "Let's get you a cake, man. On me." He flashes a twenty from a pouch inside his waistband.

A bell jingles as we open the door. Smells mix in my nose, cake, fried doughnut, boiled bagel. My mouth suds up. A display case holds cupcakes arranged on plates. *So many colors, all that frosting.* I can taste the sugar on my tongue.

Dave slaps the twenty down. "A cake for my friend."

The clerk frowns. She has blue hair today. "You want to order a cake?"

"Yeah," Dave says. "Make it say, 'Happy Birthday S-Man'."

"Ohh ... kay." The clerk takes out an order pad. Her eyebrow lifts. "Our cakes start at $29.95."

When Dave does not react, she sighs. "What kind do

you want? Chocolate? Red velvet? *Devil's* food?"

"Fuck you!" Dave erupts. He jabs his finger forward. "The Lord rebuke thee, foul temptress, instrument of Satan!"

The clerk presses a cell phone to her ear.

"It's cool," I say to the clerk. "It's cool." I wrap my arms around Dave. "Come on, let's go." I coax him through the door, and we hurry down North Street.

"Stupid," Dave mutters. "Stupid, stupid, stupid."

"It's going to be all right," I say. A siren sounds. I don't feel invisible now.

Concrete steps lead down to the right. Relief washes over me. *This is where I slept last night.* I pull Dave into the basement and close the door carefully, hoping the broken hasp won't show.

"We gotta lay low," Dave says. The whites of his eyes flash in the semi-dark. The acrid urine smell is overpowering.

"No worries," I say. "I know this place."

I unbuckle the backpack and spread the tarp into a corner. Dave leans his guitar against the wall. He sits beside me, stiff-backed with tension.

"It's cool," I murmur. "We're safe." I want to believe it's true. Dave's the one they really want. If they find us, it's Dave who is in trouble. All I have to do ... I stop that thought.

Footsteps pass. A fire truck siren sounds. Even so, I'm drifting off to sleep before I know it. That's one thing that is easier now.

The Trencher Mansion

by Gay Degani

The oaks and sycamores along the Old Road offer shade, but do nothing to alleviate the oppressive heat. Only when the hot summer sun falls behind the ridge on the other side of Riolito creek does Gus leash up Gracie and head out. It's the shadowy time of day – Gus hasn't even fixed dinner yet, waiting for sunset – so he decides not to trek down to the creek, but stick to the sidewalk. He's slow, and so is the dog, both of them old and drained of energy even though they've stayed inside all day in front of an oscillating blower fan from Walmart.

When Gus passes the Trencher mansion, he's surprised to find its faded gate gaping open. In the fading light, he squints at the yard's thick dry weeds tickling the bottom of the Shane Realty "For Sale" sign. He should tell his son to cut the grass – Mars works for that realty lady who has the listing – because if the Trencher goes up in flames, the neighboring bungalows where Gus lives won't stand a chance. Almost no rain since December, what the hell is going on with the weather? Windstorms in winter, polar vortexes back east, now severe drought in the west? "The gods," mutters Gus, "are angry."

A man in a flapping white jacket rushes down the walkway of the low-slung stucco cottage next door, aiming for Gus, setting off Gracie, who yelps and strains at her leash. The old man pulls her in and steps out of the way, but the man – the podiatrist or chiropractor, Gus can't remember which, with the pretty young wife, his brow now puckered with worry – stops and begs, "Have you seen her, a woman about your height and slender with light brown hair, maybe walking?"

"Hush, Gracie. Who? What's happened?"

The dog barks and hides behind Gus' legs.

"The front door was open, her purse on the kitchen table, but I can't find her," the man says. "Have you seen her? My wife?"

"You sure she's not taking a nap. Gracie, *heel*."

Sam Martin shakes his head and pivots away, through the open gate and across the weedy lawn, up the driveway of the Trencher house.

"Hey!" Gus hollers, "You can't go in there. Nobody's home." The old man shambles after him, Gracie trotting ahead, Gus' heart speeding up, his mind jumbled with images of the woman dead, the man breaking a window, the mansion going up in flames.

"This is private property." Gus puffs toward the backyard. He hears the younger man calling, "Charmaine!"

Plywood has been nailed over sliding doors or maybe French doors, shards of glass and splintered wood barely visible in the growing dark. The younger man rattles the kitchen doorknob. Pounds the door with the side of his fist. "Charmaine?"

Catching his breath, Gus gasps, "She – she can't be in there."

The man turns toward Gus. "She's gone in before."

"She got a key or something?"

"Well no, but she finds a way in." The younger man studies the back of the house, his eyes glancing from window to window.

Gus wonders if she's the one who broke the patio sliders. "You can't go in there. We should call the cops."

The man takes a deep breath. "Look, we live next door. My name's Sam Martin. I've seen you walking your dog. My wife, she hasn't been well."

"You're a doctor?"

"Podiatrist. She does this sometimes, disappears. She's been coming here, and I don't want to call the cops if she's sitting inside in some corner, crying."

Gus lowers his head and then shifts his eyes toward Sam Martin. Reluctantly, he says, "Okay, but I'll go in too to make sure you don't take anything."

Sam Martin nods, then strides across the patio, glass crunching under his feet, to grab a tattered lawn chair and carries it back to the house, positioning it below a window. Using the chair like a step ladder, Sam puts a foot on the front of the seat frame and his other foot on the top of the back of the chair. It wobbles, but holds his weight as he presses the bottom part of the window upward and hefts himself inside.

Sam looks down at Gus from the open window, says, "I'll let you in so you can keep an eye on me."

He ducks inside and a few seconds later the kitchen door opens. "Can you help me look? If she's not here, I need to get in my car and search the neighborhood. I don't want to waste time."

"Is there something wrong with her?"

"No – yes. She's been depressed is all and sometimes she has this urge to get away. If you can look around down here, I'll go upstairs. She's usually up in the nursery." Sam scrapes fingers through his hair.

"The nursery?"

"She miscarried in January. You can bring your dog inside."

Gus shuffles into the kitchen, though he doesn't like it much, breaking into someone else's house. Then it hits him. She was pregnant. Lost a baby. His own wife had lost one too all those years back, and they'd waited a long time before they had Mars. He feels himself softening toward the other man.

It's musty and dark inside, empty over six months, for sale for three or four. His son works for the listing agent and says she wants to sell to someone who'll turn it into a bed and breakfast, all part of her personal urban renewal plan for the area. Sniffing the stale air, Gus shakes his head. Whoever buys this place has his work cut out for him.

He peeks into the murky living room. Gracie runs her nose along the carpet at his feet. The drapes are open and the streetlights have flicked on outside, casting a blurry glow across the room. What was that by the window? A shoe catching the light?

"Hello?" His voice sounds weak and frightened to his own ears. What was her name? He clears his throat and says "hello" again, moving slowly into the room, pulling Gracie with him, cursing his old man eyes. He leans down. Grace snorts and picks up whatever it is in her mouth. He takes it from her, a crumpled bag, stinking of French fries.

Floorboards creak above his head, Gracie yelps, and he jumps. "Hell!" Dropping the bag, he hurries out of the room, not quite remembering where the kitchen is, stopping to glance into another room, dark and foreboding, with what he takes for headless shoulders at first glance, his mouth going dry, only to realize what he sees silhouetted against the window are dining room chairs.

Back into the hall, peering toward the front door and a staircase, he shouts, "Dr. Martin!"

A thundering down the stairs startles Gus. The dog lets out two sharp barks. Sam Martin arrives at the bottom, asking, "Did you find her?"

"No. Just an old French fry bag. Maybe it's hers?"

Somewhere in the dark house a door closes. Not a slam, but kind of click.

"What was –" asks Gus.

Gracie growls.

Sam hisses. "Shhh!"

Gus leans down and picks her up, clamps her muzzle, just as Sam grabs the older man's shirt and drags him to a door near the kitchen.

Sam whispers. "Wait here. Block the door." And slowly turns the knob. The door squeaks as it opens. Cool air gusts up. Stairs lead down.

Gus feels Sam's hand squeeze his shoulder and watches the young man descend into the blackness below. Gracie quivers in his arms. Gus takes one or two steps down and leans over to see what he can see. Nothing, so he takes another step. He wishes he had a flashlight, trying to do anything without –

Below there's a grunt and a scream, and the crash of glass and metal against cement and Gus is knocked against the wall, falls on his butt, a shock of pain up his tailbone, as someone rushes past him, up the steps, Gracie loosened from his grasp in hot barking pursuit. Above, running feet and Gracie's fury, then the slam of a door. Gus gasps for air, tries to pull himself up, feels a hand under his arm lifting him.

"You okay, old fellow?" asks Sam Martin.

"Gracie!" says Gus as he finds his feet.

They lumber up the stairs, the dog in the kitchen ranting at the backdoor. Sam searches for a light switch, flicks it on, but it doesn't work. He opens the door and they hasten out where a full moon glints in the glass scattered across the patio.

"Was that her?" asks Gus as he catches his breath.

Sam doesn't answer right away. He plops down onto the step, burying his head in his hands. "No. Just some kid."

Hot and light-headed, Gus pivots toward the backyard, and catches in the moonlight, just for a moment, a glimpse of his own long-dead wife.

Playing with
the Big Boys

by Sally-Anne Macomber

To: Milton Flaxmill, Red Cow Publishing
From: Trudy Polaris
Date: July 20, 2014 11:57 a.m.
Re:

I don't know what it is about you Milton but you keep me awake at night! You're like the strong silent type except you might not be so strong now because you might also be dead.

I haven't heard from you for over 6 months so your death could be a distinct possibility. And my *Nuclear Fission in The Pyrénées* manuscript could be languishing in the bottom drawer of your desk. And maybe not even yours. It could be someone else's desk. Or your old desk that's been sent down to the basement for storage. Did you make sure you cleaned out all the drawers before you sent it downstairs? Is that an official policy at Red Cow Publishing?

These are the thoughts that keep me awake at night, Milton.

(Did you see how I didn't put anything in the subject line of this email? It's because – and it feels a little weird to admit this but well, I've admitted worse things – I'm a woman of mystery.)

Yeah, who would have thought, over-communicator-of-the-century Trudy Polaris actually keeping something secret?

Well, I have a lot of secrets, Milton, I'm just very choosy who I keep them from. Because I believe in human happiness and the pursuit of generosity.

Just in case you were asking yourself that very question.

While eating lunch at your desk and editing everyone else's book but mine.

Later:
So, now it's a little later (just in case you didn't know what 'Later' on the line above meant) and I've had my little barium enema pick-me-up, but things are still a little confusing for me here in the Tyrol – oh yes! we are still heeeeere, Milton, on the world's longest tax break, but that's so depressing I don't want to talk / type / write about it for one minute one second one millisecond longer – so I'm just going to do some freefall free associating while I type instead.

So. I keep seeing mountains all the time. I look out the window and I see mountains (we *finally* ate our way through the wall of fetta, and now I can never pat a goat on the butt in quite the same way again) and I can't help thinking of the mountains I wrote about in my book – the Pyrénées, those mountains on the French-Spanish border, if you care to remember.

Oh, how do I put it without sounding a little silly?

OK. The Pyrénées are sweet enough but I can't help thinking that maybe they're just the wrong mountains for me. That is God's truth. I look at the Tyrolean Alps and think, the Pyrénées just seem ever so slightly immature in comparison. It's not their fault, it just *IS*, it's just NATURE, and you can't buck nature.

And the other day I was trolling the internet and I came across some photos of the Nepalese Royal Family and in the background were the Himalayas and I thought, those are *some* mountains, Trudy, and those mountains are truly deserving of your talents. Not those pathetic Pyrénées but those macho mountains, the Indian ones, the ones in Nepal, the ones at the top of the world.

That's really where I should be Milton, at the top of the world, not down here in Tyrolean Lego Land, but up there, with the big guys.

And then I thought, well, I bet nothing even vaguely nuclear has ever gone on up there, not in those pristine looking snow-capped mountains I thought, sipping my coffee. (I'd gone grocery shopping just the day before so we had some coffee again.) And I sighed, and my sighs last a good deal longer up here in the Alps because the air is thinner, and then my husband thought I had the hiccups and he burst into the room and pressed a gun to my head and the shock made me stop hiccupping.

(OK, that didn't happen that last bit, I'm just checking to see if you're still with me. If you are, please send me your reply in red, so I'll know you read this far.)

But these are the things that try me and I am positive they would not if I had some news from you. It's hard not being communicated with when you're a big communicator.

Later again:
I just looked it up on the internet and nothing even remotely nuclear ever happened in the Himalayas, not even close by, so I'm stuck with the Pyrénées. You are probably greatly relieved – yay, you say, no taking out *Pyrénées*

seven times from every page and replacing them all with *Himalayas* – but I can't help but feel disappointed. In fact, I just gave a big sigh and because the air really is a good deal thinner up here it really did last longer than I expected.

(I get the feeling you're not believing me Milton. Just another reason to come and visit and breathe for yourself!)

So now we come to the purpose of my email which is: the cover.

Because I can't get mountains out of my head, I'm thinking mountains might be good on the cover. I would send you some potential photos I downloaded but they're of the Himalayas – they're stalking me, those big guys, calling me to expose them! – so I wonder if we can't capture the essence of the Himalayas in the cover anyway. No one would know. It would just be subliminal, like one 25th of a second but longer and on a book cover. Just a flash of the Himalayas just to give people the idea. No one'd get hurt.

You could disguise them, of course, by moving them around. They don't all have to be of Mt Everest, you could throw in a few more of those other Himalayas too.

I like simple designs so here is a design that I am positive would probably work. You just need to make it bigger and in colour and glossy and mountainous.

(I know it doesn't look much but I'm really more after their *essence*.)

The latest Later:
I think I have been spelling 'fetta' when really it should be 'feta'. This is why I loathe spelling anything.

If you are going over some of my older emails to you, could you correct that please?

Up the Himalayas!

Trudy

To: Leonard Strauss Jr., Red Cow Publishing
From: Trudy Polaris
Date: July 20, 2014 1:32 p.m.
Re: !!!!!!!!!!!!!!!!!!!!!!!

Frohe Weihnachten, Herr Strauss!

What a coincidence that I should be talking to Frau Erdbeeren just yesterday in the Fleischerei and she mentioned she has a brother in Boston … who works in publishing … and at Red Cow Publishing, no less … as the Dialect Editor / Janitor!

I was immediately struck by your job title – though less by the words *dialect* and *editor* and more by the word *janitor*.

I am wondering if you have a key to the basement where the editing staff keep all their old office furniture. And if you could look through the drawers of the old desk of Milton Flaxmill? And rescue a manuscript of mine that I am sure is gathering dust in the bottom drawer.

The manuscript is called *Nuclear Fission in the Pyrénées* (since renamed *Nuclear Fission in The Pyrénées*) and I would be eternally grateful if you could find it, read it, cross out every mention of the word *Pyrénées*, and replace them all with the word *Himalayas*.

Doing the same on the title page would be good too. Though please keep my name – Trudy Polaris – wherever it is mentioned.

(I have not seen one example of messy Austrian penmanship since we moved to the Tyrol earlier this year in a bid to improve our tax standing, so I am sure you would do all the crossing-out and adding-in in a neat and steady hand.)

Then please take the manuscript up to Milton Flaxmill's desk and put it in his In-Tray.

I'm sure his old desk is there in the basement.

As you will see by all the exclamation marks in the Subject of this email, my request is very important.

It's been a terrible and stressful last few months (perhaps Frau Erdbeeren has already spoken of me?) but I am determined to put all this negativity behind me and move forward, ready to embrace the anticipation of my success.

There is also the added incentive of a financial reward for your troubles. I can cut you in on an amazing Europe-wide gourmet cheese distribution deal.

Speed is of the essence here too, so just a quick message telling me you received this email, took the elevator (or *lift*, as I usually say) down to the basement, found the desk, unlocked the bottom drawer, pulled out the manuscript, changed all the mentions of *Pyrénées* to *Himalayas* including the title page (and in a neat and steady hand), then took it upstairs and deposited it in Milton Flaxmill's In-Tray, would be good.

If you are speaking with Frau Erdbeeren soon, please thank her for me, and tell her I have contacted you. She seemed very concerned that I did so, and I would hate her to think I had not followed up on her good advice.

Given the possibility that Milton Flaxmill may have left the building, left Red Cow Publishing, left Boston or even left this mortal earth, what do you suggest would be a wise next step in that eventuation?

Thanking you in advance, for a job well done!

Grüß Gott,

Frau Trudi Polaris

Discipline

by Mandy Nicol

"I knew Persephone would like the Colonel," says Mum, feeding another sliver of KFC to the Pomeranian perched on her lap at the dining room table.

"I thought the chicken was for you," I say. "I thought you wanted it for lunch. *Your* lunch. I wouldn't have gone out of my way to get it for the bloody dog." Seph licks Mum's fingers clean and I stand beside the table, ready to scoop the spoilt little mutt off the table if she decides to help herself to her special meal.

"There's no need to speak like that Nadia, and it was a small detour off the highway. How much did it add to your trip back from Melbourne, five minutes?" Mum wipes her fingers with a serviette, then uses it to delicately dab around Seph's mouth.

"It was more like half an hour, actually." I tear some meat off a drumstick for Peregrine, drooling and overlooked under the table. "It wouldn't normally bother me but I have to finish embroidering the logos on all those shirts for the pub. They want them tomorrow."

"Well that's not my fault."

"I didn't say it was, but ..."

Mum slaps her hands on the table. "If you'd listened to me you'd have had plenty of time to do the shirts! You'd have been here instead of gadding about in the city with

Charlie all weekend. You can't run around like a teenager and expect your business to look after itself, Nadia."

She pauses for breath. She's yanked me off cloud nine and I turn to escape but I'm too late, she starts up again.

"Now, if you had your brother's business sense you might get away with it, but with the best will in the world you're no business manager and you never will be, so if you're running behind, don't blame me." She shakes her head. "We all told you at the start that you'd have to treat it like a business and not some fancy little hobby you pick up and put down as you please. Discipline, that's what it needs, and if things are falling apart that's what it'll come down to, so you can quit blaming me."

I stare at her for a good ten seconds. "Nothing's falling apart, Mum, and I'm not blaming you for anything." I step into the kitchen and take her pill box off the fridge, make sure the Monday compartment is empty. I don't like it when her face turns beetroot. "How about a nice cup of tea?" I call out, flicking the switch on the kettle.

"No thank you, I wouldn't dare waste any more of your precious time."

"All right then." I turn the kettle off. I'd much rather immerse myself in memories of the weekend.

I scarper down the hall to my workroom, which is actually the spare room, which means I get to hear her talk to the dogs about how I never listen, how I'll never learn, and how I'll be sorry when she's dead.

I pick up the box of shirts waiting for their logos.

And I wonder about that sorry bit.

Heat Rises

by Margaret Bingel

July in the city is a humid, sticky time of the year, but the weathermen claim the heat wave should be over in a few days. Ned and his mother are drinking iced tea while standing in the back doorway of his apartment, Ned with one foot on the back stoop, his mother's head sticking just outside. Nadia gnaws on an ice cube, belly flat on the kitchen linoleum.

"Ned, I wish you'd get an air conditioner. This weather is no good for a dog. Look at her," Nora points to the dog, now growling as she tries to crack the cube. "Dogs don't sweat, you know. You should take better care of her."

"Mom, she's fine," Ned says, keeping his eyes on the waves of heat undulating the sunset. "I keep her watered, she pees a lot, it's alright."

"Watered? Ned, she's not a plant!"

He rolls his eyes. She needs to stop panicking, he thinks as he steps back inside to get more tea from the fridge. His mother follows him to the kitchen, still talking.

"Have you been taking her out on walks every day? Have you been remembering to feed her? How is your physical therapy, is she keeping you on your feet? You know you have to keep moving every day or else your muscles will atrophy again, and you don't want that, now do you?"

Ned pours more iced tea into their glasses. He puts the pitcher back in the fridge.

"And how is work going? Are you still able to work? It's ok to push yourself, but not that hard."

"Mom, I work as a translator for a juicer company. It's not like I'm going to get finger strain typing Spanish. And since I work from home, there's no need for me to leave the house unless I'm going to the store, or if I have to take Nadia out on a walk."

Hearing her name, Nadia lifts her head to her owner, and wags her tail. If Nadia could have human thoughts, with words instead of pictures, she'd tell him that he left the fridge door open again. Instead, she steps away from her ice cube and nudges Ned.

In the month he's had her, Ned's memory hasn't grown better so much as it's now easier to prompt him when he's forgotten something. Figuring she must've been a service dog school drop-out, he has no other explanation for Nadia's intelligence and intuition for when he's misplaced objects, left his shoes untied, and now, left a door open. Every time she pokes him with her nose, Ned picks up on his mistakes.

After closing the door and patting Nadia on the head, his mother asks, "Why aren't you seeing a therapist for your depression?"

He looks his mother full in the face. Ned can't tell her that he prefers suicide to therapy, and the last thing he needs is another chattering harpy in his life not listening to him.

"Mom," Ned starts, "you need a man in your life and you need to leave me alone."

Nora places her glass of iced tea on the kitchen counter and leaves before he can say anymore. When he hears his front door snap shut, he wonders if he said too much. But she needed to hear that, he rationalizes. He faces his kitchen window and looks out at the sunset.

All That Trouble

by Darryl Price

Hey, Doc, did you hear? They tell me I'm going home pretty soon. Probably next week, next week sometime. I won't know what to do with myself.

I'm going to miss you, Doc. You've been a real good friend to me, which to all but us chickens seems like a funny kind of thing to say to someone in your position, I know, but I mean it. You've kept the fox at bay.

Well, this isn't the final goodbyes or anything remotely like that, or is it, nope this is just the same old routine point of the day where I tell you all the things I've been meaning to express this week, like always. What are you going to do with all those papers, Doc? Burn them?

It's going to be lonely.

You know I started one of these yesterday but it got accidentally thrown out, so now I keep them under my pillow – for safekeeping.

It was something to do with the moon. Oh yeah I think I kind of remember it now. It's when I got in trouble with your staff for chasing the moon that one night. I don't know. It just seemed like the right thing to do then. The moon was so big and bright and I needed that kind of company, so I went outside to get a closer look, but the moon's a tricky customer, Doc. Just when you think you'll be able to tap her on the shoulder and ask her name she appears somewhere else, higher, farther away. It's

103

frustrating. Still I was attracted to that particular moon that night for sure and felt like I had to go to her. So I did. I didn't mean to cause all that crazy trouble. In the end it was more trouble for me than anybody else because I had to swallow all those pills and be watched every second of the rest of the night. I felt like a dog chained to a doghouse. And I still never met that particular moon maiden, if you know what I mean. Maybe one doesn't so much get to meet the moon as be allowed in its presence. Jesus, that's a lonely thought there.

Well, anyway, I do appreciate all your help. I know I'm going to be just fine. It might be a little rough in the beginning – because really I don't want to have to talk with anybody, but what if someone asks me a question? I guess I'll have to deal with that as it comes.

I've got a little money saved up, a little money left, so I should be able to buy some groceries and pay the electric bill.

Do you think I'll ever be happy, Doc?

Maybe I should get a dog.

Thursday

24

July
2014

Quelle Surprise

by Teresa Burns Gunther

Rachel unfolds from the cab at Pier 39. It's July 24th. 6:00 pm. San Francisco has wrapped her gray shawl around the day, dropping the temperature into the 50s. Susie's not waiting in front of the Aquarium as agreed. Rachel grits her teeth and texts *where r u?* Susie responds *w/the seals!* Rachel passes shivering tourists along the wooden wharf. Screeching seagulls swoop for easy pickings. A juggler packs up his machetes and bowling balls while a homeless man terrifies tourists with his outstretched, distressed hand; a kid who needs voice lessons entertains Japanese tourists with a red guitar, the case begging.

Susie appeared last night as Rachel stepped into the bath. She'd worked late at the office parsing the tax return of a faux investor-lawyer who secreted pilfered millions into phony accounts he created using his daughter's SSN. Rachel peeked through the curtains to find her cousin with suitcases on the porch. *Damn.*

"Surprise!" Susie shouted, hair hacked all different lengths like she'd had an argument with a blender.

"We don't want any," Rachel said, holding Stella whose barks became whimpers of joy. *Traitor.* "Why are you here?"

"Visiting. Remember? I called."

"Yes. And I said no."

"Rach," Susie laughed as she wrestled her bags inside. "You're so funny!"

Rachel knew she should tell Susie to leave. Her last visit involved a party while Rachel was working that left her apartment a mess, the liquor cabinet empty, and jewelry gone missing. But, Susie is 50% of her remaining family tree.

"One night, Susie. No guests."

Rachel finds Susie ogling sea lions with two men in tow. She's 27, a fluttery package of curves. Her hacked hair dyed an odd "champagne" color stands on end in a frigid wind that drags the evening into the 40s. Rachel made Susie leave the house with her this morning, planning to meet for a goodbye dinner after work. Susie's dressed the part of tourist in shorts and goose bumps, her lips colorless with cold. She's bouncing on her toes, hands fluttering as she talks, acting out a story starring herself. When they were kids Susie's stories tricked Rachel into believing Susie was exciting, complex. But she's learned that her cousin is like the Russian nesting dolls Rachel's father sent in lieu of a 7th birthday visit. When taken apart, the dolls reveal themselves in new costumes, growing smaller and smaller, to their baby core. Susie adopts different personas but when you get to the heart of her there's just a little girl incapable of organizing herself into a woman's life. Rachel's heel drops into a crack in the walkway; she wrestles it free, regretting agreeing to meet at Fisherman's Wharf, a tourist trap she usually avoids.

Susie introduces Rachel to her catch, farm boys from Indiana. Steve is short, buff and tan with hair and teeth bleached white. He's wearing crisp jams, sandals, and a tight *Frisco* sweatshirt. He's an actor working his way to LA and stardom. Kevin is tall and lives in San Francisco. He looks like a farmer; lean, square-jawed and freckled in jeans and leather jacket; a software engineer.

"Don't tell anyone," Kevin says. Young techies are the latest whipping boy for SF's housing shortage and skyscraping rents.

The sea lions stink but Susie, like Steve, is enchanted. "They're *so* cute!" She hops, pink sneakers slapping the wharf. Susie's "between jobs," a space she occupies more each year. She has little money but probably paid a fortune for her huge tourist sweatshirt, identical to Steve's. She links arms with Rachel, who towers over her, and poses on tiptoe for Steve to take her picture while Kevin slyly checks out Rachel's legs. "Oh Steve! Thank you!" Susie beams, like he's just cured Ebola and turns the camera on him. "Give me your number and I'll text these to you." She winks at Rachel and whispers, "You can have the tall one." Susie promised to find Rachel "a manhunk" before leaving town. Given Susie's penchant for guys with compasses set south of trouble Rachel suggested she leave well enough alone. Her resolution for July is *be open to new experiences* but Susie's *surprise!* slammed that door last night.

"I just have to pet those seals!" Susie says, looking for a way onto the floating haul outs.

"They're *sea lions,* and wild, and protected. They can be nasty," Rachel says, but Susie waves her off. "Excuse her," Rachel tells the guys. "She's judgment impaired."

"See!" Susie says. "I told you Rachel has a great sense of humor!"

Rachel shakes her head. "You know that's code for *my friend's a dog,* right?"

Kevin, *the tall one*, throws his head back and laughs, a rib-rattling *hahaha*. It wasn't that funny. "That's what *I* was figuring." He wipes his eyes. "But you're not. A dog. I mean

..." He coughs. "You're ..." He shoves his hands in his pockets and turns pink.

"Very attractive?" Rachel suggests.

He smiles, saved. "Yeah."

"Thank you." Rachel gives him the once-over. Her gaydar says he's straight.

"Isn't it amazing, they're cousins too. And from Indiana, like me?" Susie says, like this meet-up's on Mars. "We should celebrate!"

"I have work to do." Rachel points to her watch.

"Well, we have to eat." She clutches Steve's and Kevin's arms. "All four of us!"

Outside the Crab Pot restaurant, Susie frowns at the menu. "I don't know." She taps a long, green fingernail against her teeth. "It's mostly crab." She makes snapping pincers of her fingers.

"Quelle surprise!" Rachel says. "Are you allergic?"

"No."

"Vegetarian?"

Susie lifts her chin. "I'm a cutetarian."

Rachel won't ask.

Steve the actor does.

"It means I only eat *cute* animals."

"How weird of you," Rachel says.

Susie strikes a pose and waves a hand over herself. "Well ... you are what you eat!"

Kevin laughs like she's a riot.

Steve claps. "I just love that!" He's not even acting.

"Maybe," Rachel says, "we can find you some deep fried kitties."

Steve looks alarmed, but Kevin grins. He's getting better-looking.

Inside, fishing nets with faux crab and lobster drape the restaurant walls. When the waiter comes to their booth Susie says, "Four Cosmos, please."

"Coffee for me," Rachel says. "Remember, we agreed it's an early night?"

"I'll have McCallan, neat," Kevin says. That's Rachel's drink. He takes off his leather jacket. His T-shirt says *"You can shoot yourself in the foot in any language, C++ allows you to reuse the bullet."* This makes Rachel laugh, which earns her another grin. "Most people," Kevin says, sliding closer, "don't get it."

Rachel stands before the restroom mirror and smooths her dark hair, pleased at how smart she looks in her fitted blue suit. But if she's so smart why is Susie staying another night? The door flies open. Clearly Susie thinks bathroom visits are a group activity.

"Kevin likes you," Susie says, touching up her lipstick. "Admit it. I did good! Found us each a man our size." She laughs at this, her eyes bright. Their dark blue color is the only proof they share DNA. "Steve's so hot, and an actor!" she says, like this is a rare find. "You must feel it."

"Feel what?"

"The chemistry." Susie puckers her lips and smiles, delighted, perhaps at some new idea of herself. Rachel just nods, sad to think Susie might never turn her enthusiasm to some true and lasting effort. Like what? Rachel mocks herself, a mortgage? Working for the IRS?

Susie steps close, serious now.

"I know we didn't have much time together Rach, but I've agreed to drive Steve to LA." As if fearful Rachel might argue, she adds, "He's paying for gas."

Rachel thinks she should talk Susie out of it. It's clear she's clueless that Steve's gay. But her face is so bright, so full of hope. Rachel tries to remember the last time she opened herself up to that.

Morgana Malone and the Mystery of the Manna from Heaven

by Matt Potter

"Morgana Malone?"

I turn and see a young man, high cheekbones on a thin face and short dark hair atop deep brown eyes. He's looking at me through the open driver's window of a shiny, dark blue car. It's cold and the sky above is that depressing pale grey we all grow to know and loathe over the Australian winter. No rain, just cold and grey and dull dull dull. But it's a quiet suburban neighbourhood and we appear to be the only two people around – me on the footpath and he in his car with the engine still running in the middle of the street.

I stuff the leaflets back into my cotton hold-all – it's too cold to do two things at once – while I talk to this charming man. I want to know how he knows me.

"Morgana?" he asks, his eyebrows aquiver. And he smiles. "You must be, it's your hair, it's so ... *orange.*"

I brush my hair with my hand, which is past my shoulders now, but it unsettles the beanie on top of my head – I hate beanies but it's keeping my head warm – and the hat falls to the ground. So I bend down, and the cowl neck of the thick jumper looped across my chest swoops down in front as I pick the beanie up off the footpath.

He lets out a large whistle. "Whoa! It *is* you, that racing stripe is so sexy!"

I stand up and do the usual cramming of the beanie on my head, pulling it down over the grey-brown regrowth. I want to have my hair dyed again by a professional hairdresser – as opposed to an amateur – but it's taking a while to earn the money. And I've had a lot of bad luck job-wise (and bad luck life-wise) since I stopped working as junior admin officer at Grigor's therapy practice way back in ... oh, April ... and then Ludmilla moved out and moved in with her kitchenhand cousin Sergei and then –

"No, don't cover it up," he says, "that stripe is hot! Opi was right, you are one sexy mama." Leaning his elbow on the window frame, he grins. He has no gaps in his teeth.

When I stepped outside this morning to deliver more junk mail – my savings are running out and I don't have any other job and it gets me out in the fresh (cold, dull dull dull) air and I get a lot of knuckle exercise with all the folding beforehand plus I thought it would be a good way to meet single men – I had not expected the third degree (if this is the third degree, though, it could be the first, second or fourth degree instead) from a young man with short dark hair, deep brown eyes and all those teeth who also knows my name and who also might be single.

But I can't help it, it comes from nowhere. "I'm probably as old as your mother."

"Yeah?" He reaches forward and the engine stops idling. (He must want to talk to me, he's stopped dead in the middle of the street.) "How old would that be?" he says, and settles back into the seat.

"Forty-seven," I say. "Today, in fact. I'm forty-seven today."

"Yeah? Dang, me too! It's my birthday today as well. I'm twenty-three."

I pull the strap of my hold-all further on to my shoulder. "It's really your birthday today?"

"Nah, just kidding," he says, and grins again. This guy, he's a great grinner.

"Me too, I'm just kidding too," I say, though it actually *is* my birthday today, and I *am* forty-seven now. I'm just trying to forget. "Do you want me for something?"

"Are you busy?"

Am I busy? Well, I could be busy, I think, wondering what his plans are. If he's stalking me then yes, I'm definitely busy. But if he wants to get to know me and buy me a drink and whisk me away to somewhere that's sunny and warm and not dull dull dull grey, then no, I might not be so busy after all.

"Well, I'm stuffing letterboxes with advertising for *Knights of the Polish Cross* sauvignon blanc," I say, half-flashing him a tri-fold leaflet sticking out of my hold-all, "if that counts as *busy*." I step off the kerb and hold-all swinging against my hip, cross the three metres to the car.

"Opi is right – you are a *damn* fine woman, Morgana Malone."

I'm standing by the driver's door now, hands in the pockets of my corduroy trousers. "Who's Opi?"

"Opi. You know, Julius Rubinstein, from where you used to work." But he says it Germanically, *Yoo-lee-ess*. Yoo-lee-ess Roo-bin-shtine.

"Oh, Mr Rubinstein!" I smile, happy to remember my favourite patient at Grigor's therapy practice, and I rock back on my heels. "No one can carry off an eye patch and toupée quite the way he can. How is he?"

"Good," he says. "Okay," he says. "Well, not too good really," he says. "A bit fucked."

Mr Rubinstein is sitting up in bed, his toupée perched further back on his head so it looks like it's revving up for a take-off, and his eye patch removed, a darkened sewn-up hole where his eye once was. A nurse holds his wrist with one hand and with her watch in the other, checks his pulse. Which strikes me as old-fashioned (isn't there a robot to do this?) but then, with a toupée and eye patch and all, Mr Rubinstein is an old-fashioned kind of man.

"It is lovely to see you, my dahlink," he says, smiling against the pillows. "You and your lovely orange hair, just like my late, dear wife."

"And it's lovely to see you, too," I say, but it's not. A tube reaches in through his left nostril and a drip is attached to his right arm. And his skin is grey, near to translucent, and it's the middle of winter and a little chilly on the ward but sweat beads on his forehead, and his arms and the skin stretched across his collarbone are shiny with sweat. Even in the short time since I last saw him – an everyday sight until I left the job in late April – he's older and thinner and frailer and closer to the end.

I sniff and the room smells of sickly-sweet old man sweat but I smile at him anyway. I don't know whether to kiss his cheek or hold his other hand or what, so I just stand at the end of the bed. Which allows Seth – his grandson, the one who found me walking the streets delivering *Knights of the Polish Cross* junk mail – time to open the folder at the end of the bed and glance over his medical notes.

"My grandson is makink sure I have the best care in the hospital," Mr Rubinstein says. "He is a *brilliant* medical student and he will be a *brilliant* doctor. But seeink you is the best medicine, my dear, always the *best*."

I smile again. I'm smiling but I don't know what else to do. There's no reception desk separating us and now I'm just the visitor, not the person printing invoices and picking up the 'phone and doing all the things Zebadie didn't have the insight or interest to do. I'm just someone who was picked up on the street by a man half her age and whisked in for a visit.

The nurse returns Mr Rubinstein's hand to the mattress and taking the medical file from Seth's grasp, opens it on the tray table beside the bed and scribbles inside the folder.

"It's Morgana's birthday, Opi," Seth says, ignoring the nurse. And he winks at me.

"How old are you today, my dear? Not a day over twenty-two!"

"Forty-seven," I say. And to Seth I say, "Actually, it *is* my birthday."

"Yeah, I know," Seth adds. "It's *my* birthday too."

Mr Rubinstein yawns, his mouth full of big yellow teeth and a furry, white tongue.

"You need to drink more, Opi," Seth says. "Keep your fluids up."

The nurse wheels the tray table over Mr Rubinstein's legs, and taking a plastic cup filled with water and a straw from the bedside cabinet, plonks it down on the tray table.

"I just thought you might like a visitor, Opi," Seth says. And then to me, "Opi talks about you a lot."

"You need to keep your fluids up, Mr Rubinstein," the nurse says, patting his leg. Then she slots the medical notes back in their wire cage at the end of the bed and, white shoes squeaking on the lino, walks out of the room.

Mr Rubinstein opens his eyes wide and lifts up his arms, as if beholding something. "Such a vision," he says, I think to me.

"She was hard to track down," Seth says.

"You must come back and visit me when I am feelink better," Mr Rubinstein adds. And closes his eyes. Then he opens one, just a little. "Beauty always makes me feel better."

"Was I really that hard to track down?" I ask, as we walk out onto North Terrace to the beeping horns and gear changes of Friday mid-afternoon traffic. "Did you have to go to the police or scour the 'phone book or the electoral roll or dental records?"

I look at Seth side-on – high cheekbones on a thin face and short dark hair atop deep brown eyes. And am struck by how much he looks like Grigor. And he's a doctor too.

"No," says Seth, looking into my eyes and grinning again. "Wanna go back to my place for a birthday fuck?"

Hazard

by Gary Percesepe

Seven months after his divorce, a man steers his rented Cadillac Seville down the narrow lane of a manicured country club, positions the car so that it is facing the eighteenth green, and cuts the engine. He touches a button and four windows glide down leather doors, letting in the local air, and with it, a flood of memories.

Playing alone on a sultry July afternoon at his New England club, Gary Hollow had it at one under par on the thirteenth hole when it occurred to him that his wife may be having an affair. Dropping his bag to the ground, he fished a clean white handkerchief from one of the side pockets, and blotted his brow. Just yesterday, one of his firm's senior partners had remarked that he was mildly surprised at how reasonable Savannah had been. They had been in the library in the tort section, researching negligence in the Shinnecock tribe case. Gary started to speak, he'd been filling the air with explanations and aimed to continue, but Vanderslice placed his hand gently on his shoulder and said, "Son, save it. You've made the common mistake of thinking your divorce is interesting."

He and Savannah had been best friends in college. They were part of a touring Princeton ensemble that performed at the tall steeple Congregational churches of Vermont and New Hampshire. Savannah was a soprano, he a baritone, part of a group of eight perfectly matched voices that sang French madrigals and holiday music. Gary was taken in by Savannah's long, willowy frame, accentuated by a floor length cross-back jersey maxi which she had toughened up with a military parka and Doc Martens. With her pancake makeup and thick mascara, Savannah looked like Morticia Addams, had Morticia been a blonde. It was a joke between them, Gary holding her pale arm aloft in the Princeton touring van, kissing it in two inch intervals as the others cheered, and he proclaimed to her, only half joking, "Cara Mia!"

Gary placed the handkerchief back in his bag, pulled his driver, and stepped onto the manicured tee box. As he rehearsed his swing and tried to visualize the way he must shape his next shot, he saw instead Savannah in her skinny jeans, and then the way she applied night cream to her pretty face before climbing into bed next to him. One day soon that stops, Gary thought. And someone else will watch her move in those jeans, through the Italian restaurant or pottery shop and into her car, into the seat beside him, knowing at the end of the day he can remove them from her slim hips and watch her apply her night cream and count the seconds till she presents herself to him in bed.

He placed a white tee into the ground and wondered, how had they come to this? Just last month, lying in bed on a Sunday morning, he and Savannah had rehearsed a half dozen scenarios – married too early, two miscarriages, Gary's meddlesome mother who had never approved of her son's wife's couture, the numbing routine of a young New England associate at an historic Boston firm, with longer and longer nights at the office and fewer opportunities to spend time together. When they spoke of these things that Sunday, their tone was one of sweet reason, doctor conferring with lawyer, as if they had simply missed a question on their SATs. Married young, divorced young. They would both go on. She in pediatric medicine, he at the firm. It was far from tragic. With all that was terribly wrong in this violent crazed irrational world, their problems didn't amount to much, even to them. They would use a mediator, one not from his firm. They would go on as best pals. No fault, win win, the ideal way to play it.

Gary smashed his drive, starting it over the right side of the fairway, a high arcing draw. He shouldered his bag and tried to reason things out. If Savannah was really having an affair, everything changes. But why? Because deceit alters things. But why? Why should it matter to him? The marriage is over. Yes, but facts matter. But if she denied an affair, he would have to establish the facts, which means an investigation. Does he want that? What if nothing happened? What are the grounds of his divorce, now? Is there a case that can be built?

He reached his ball. It had landed in the middle of the fairway, 270 yards from the tee box. He has 150 yards to the back of the green where the pin is tucked in the far left corner, guarded by a large bunker. A sucker pin placement. Gary took his stance over the ball, made a few waggles with his eight iron. He concentrated on the shot before him, a shot he had executed a hundred times or more.

But he had a corrupt swing thought, disturbed by the nagging suspicion that Savannah is seeing someone at work, and he came over the top on the shot, slicing the ball into the trees. He walked angrily after his Titleist. It had come to rest two inches from a tall maple. Trees line the right edge of the fairway on this old Donald Ross course, and he was in jail. With no other option, he took a five iron, punched out into the fairway, chipped onto the green, and two putted. Double bogey. Just like that, one over par.

Gary pulled his ball angrily from the cup and walked briskly to the ball washer at the fourteenth hole, a long par five. He pumped the ball up and down in the bright red washer, trying to remember the name of the guy Savannah had mentioned a few months back, a young intern at Boston General, the brother of one of her partners. Or was it a nephew? A guy who'd shown up with his stethoscope and blood pressure kit in a red and yellow Sesame Street lunchbox. What was his name? Halverson or Halverton. One of those. He had met him, Gary recalled. It was at an office party when he picked Savannah up at work one night when her car was in the shop. Deferential as hell, this kid doctor had been, he remembered that.

He took the ball, dimpled and gleaming white from the washer, and promptly dropped it into a small patch of mud. Cursing, he washed the ball again and placed it, still wet, in his pants pocket. On the tee box, he took a few rehearsal swings, smooth and rhythmic, and addressed his ball. He hated the thought that something had been hidden. That he had been so *not knowing*. He was not vigilant enough with Savannah, then hadn't bothered to put up a real fight for her. But why? Why had he allowed this Sesame Street kid to come between them? He had failed to *defend* her!

Sotto voce, he hummed the Emperor's Waltz. Imagining himself gliding alone around a polished dance floor, he took the club back slowly, loaded his weight onto his back leg and haunches, and made a full turn. But his right elbow flew open and he sliced again, his ball peeling like a banana and landing in the next fairway. He hit a smothered hook from the rough, managing somehow to reach the green in regulation, but then three putts from thirty feet. Furious with himself, he took his bogey and moved to the fifteenth hole.

Where he had a revelation. If Savannah *is* having an affair with Halverson or Halverton then she has surrendered to him the moral high ground.

All through their marriage Savannah had been the faithful one, the one whose steadiness guided their marriage, the one who had sacrificed her career while he advanced at the firm, the whimsical wife turned reluctant scold, who had tried to make babies while falling behind the pace in med school. And of course! It made sense that she was now the very soul of reason, now that she had proven unfaithful at last. But now he knew!

Sensing his advantage, and with the natural rhythm he had mastered as the captain of the Princeton golf team for two seasons, Gary kept his left foot grounded on the turf, felt his spikes grab and hold, his lower body stable and quiet, while he rotated his upper body in a powerful coil and lashed at the ball, unleashing a beauty, a long powerful draw that split the fairway 290 yards out.

He struck a perfect approach shot to the center of the green and drained the five footer for birdie. Back to one over par.

He birdied the next two holes and arrived at the eighteenth hole one under par. The eighteenth is a long par four, uphill, to a green that cants from top to bottom. It is important to keep the ball below the hole on the approach shot. Too deep and one finds oneself in a steep greenside bunker where it is impossible to get the ball up and down. Gary Hollow cranked a soaring drive up the fairway. His ball came to rest 160 yards from the pin, where the fairway meets the first cut of rough on the left side.

There was grass between his club and the ball. Not a good lie. Gary placed his gleaming seven iron behind the ball, hovering it over the grass, careful not to ground the club. He rehearsed what he would say to Savannah when he got home, all possible ways into his conversation about Halverson or Halverston. Halliburton! Ha! He waggled his club and tried to visualize the shot. He saw the lovely form of his wife, naked under the sheets, the sheets of Halliburton, the line of her long legs beneath the thin percales, the look of ecstasy on her face, and backed away from the shot. He shook his head and tried to empty it of every thought. Let the nothingness enter your shots, he recalled his Princeton coach say. The swing is the man. Relax, and feel it.

But as he built his stance and addressed the ball, his swing thoughts again were banished by the thought that he once had a wife and now he does not. The simple logic of subtraction: two minus one. Gary recalled the look on Savannah's face when he presented to her on their first anniversary a diamond necklace with matching earrings. He had taken care with its purchase, scouring the stores at the mall trying to find something that would fit his law school budget. The young woman who had wrapped the gift in silver striped paper had beamed up at him and told him what a perfect selection he had made for his wife. His *wife*! How proud he had been of that word, how delighted he was with Savannah, the way she moved around their small apartment, carrying toward him two gold-rimmed teacups she had found at a church rummage sale, their tiny treasures. One morning, he'd carelessly dropped one into the sink, breaking the handle. Late for court, he'd thrown the cup in the trash. That night he came home to Savannah seated at the kitchen table, holding the cup and a tube of epoxy. Were you going to tell me? she'd said.

He flailed at the ball, his swing ugly as a collapsing lawn chair, and caught it thin. Too much club and he'd airmailed the green. From where he stood, looking unsteadily from his moistened eyes, he could not tell if the ball had found the bunker. If he managed to land it in the grass beside the trap he could still save his par.

Gary Hollow trudged up the fairway to the green, stabbing at his eyes. Captain of his golf team, student government president, rising young associate sure to make partner, he understood nevertheless that he had lost Savannah. When he confronts her about Halverson – over what, a Sesame Street lunchbox? – she will look at him, in that way that she does, smile her Morticia smile, and say, "Gary, you are so sweetly dumb."

Now, alone at dusk in the gleaming white Cadillac, Gary remembers that day as if he has never left it. He scans the eighteenth green, as he had scanned it that day, raking his club through the tall grass, hoping for a break. Overhead, a lone red-tailed hawk had soared, its broad wings beating, searching its quarry. As he'd reached the crest of the hill that day, Gary saw his ball at last, sitting like a poached egg, buried in the hazard.

In the Bathroom
at Arby's

by Nathaniel Tower

It's been a month since Samford discovered he wasn't a clone. Unless of course the doctor was lying, but Samford saw no reason why he would. Since watching the doctor die in front of him, he has been on the run. He hasn't spent two nights in the same city. Today he is in Nashville, taking a shit in an Arby's bathroom. Greasy food has always sent Samford straight to the shitter, and he hasn't been able to eat anything that isn't greasy for the past month.

Samford had been eating his meal, a regular roast beef sandwich with curly fries, when his bowels started to churn. He ditched the sandwich but grabbed the box of fries and headed to the bathroom as fast as he could, clenching his cheeks on the way. He didn't even have time to line the seat with toilet paper before plopping his hairy ass down on the black rim. The shit flew right out, like a barrage of missiles out of a big ass cannon. It would've been humiliating had anyone been in there at the time. Luckily, it is 3 in the morning and listening to Samford take a putrid shit in an Arby's bathroom is the last thing on anyone's mind.

Samford's still hungry as hell, maybe even hungrier now that his bowels have been cleansed by the grease invasion, but he wants to clean the outside of his ass before introducing more fries to his system. With the curly fry box still clutched in his right hand, Samford prepares to wipe, hoping the single-ply toilet paper will be adequate for removing the fresh mess. As he peels off a piece of toilet paper, he feels the roughness with his fingers and wonders if maybe it will rub the serial number right out of his ass.

The doctor's revelation has bugged the shit out of him for the last month. Why would they put a serial number on all the non-clones? What is the purpose of this tracking? And just how extensive is the tracking? Does someone know he's taking a shit in an Arby's bathroom while holding onto his curly fries at this very moment?

The door swings open and pounds against the tile wall. If the door had opened with less force, Samford probably wouldn't have heard it. But this noise is impossible not to hear, and so Samford hears it and opts to delay his wiping. Instead, he lifts his ankle-trousered legs as high into the air as he can. He isn't sure what there is to be paranoid about. It's an Arby's bathroom. People use it to piss or shit. That's all there is to it.

Samford listens as the person he presumes to be a man unzips his pants. A gentle waterfall trickle of urine pings against the porcelain of the urinal, like the man has some kind of kidney or prostate problem. Surely the man can hear Samford's strained breathing if Samford can hear such a delicate tinkle.

The toilet flushes and the pants zip back up. The sound of water gushing from the sink comes next, followed by the roar of the hand dryer, one of those high efficiency ones. It occurs to Samford then that he hasn't heard any footsteps. This bothers him to no end. No one walks around silently in an Arby's bathroom at 3 AM. Not unless there is some serious reason to remain silent.

In spite of Samford's incredible feeling of unease, he decides to take a bite out of one of the few remaining curly fries. He can't resist. Those fries are just that good. Besides, the hand dryer will drown out the sound.

The moment that Samford's teeth clamp down on the crisp seasoned fry, the stall door kicks open. Samford sees a mirror image of himself standing right in front of him, a curly fry clenched between the man's teeth.

"What the fuck, man? How 'bout some privacy?" Samford mumbles through his fry-ridden mouth.

Samford is neither embarrassed nor afraid. He recognizes the man immediately. It's that stupid bastard who'd been in bed with him and the woman with the clone brochure. This is the first time Samford has seen this man for six months, and Samford is again appalled by just how ugly he is.

"Wipe your ass and get up," the fake Samford says.

"You're a clone, aren't you?" Samford asks.

"I said wipe your ass and get up."

Samford leans to the left and begins wiping with his right hand. The grease-soaked cardboard slides through his buttcrack and the remaining fries spill into the toilet.

The clone laughs. "You dumb ass. Wipe with the TP, not the fries. I swear. You reals have no clue sometimes."

This is the first time Samford has been called a *real*. It's the first time he's heard the term. Even when he was training for the clone Olympics, such a word was never used. Suddenly, Samford wonders if he was the only real in the clone Olympics.

Samford lets the box fall into the toilet and starts wiping with the toilet paper. He winces as the rough paper scraps across his delicate flesh. He wonders if clones have problems like this.

"Hurry up. Your ass doesn't have to be immaculate. Let's go."

The clone grabs Samford and pulls him off the toilet even though there is much wiping still to be done.

"Where are we going?" Samford asks as he is dragged out of the stall, his pants around his ankles and his junk flopping like a bloated fish out of water. The clone continues to pull Samford, not allowing him to snatch up his pants as they exit the bathroom and enter the Arby's dining area. It doesn't matter though. There are no diners. The cute girl with the nose piercing behind the counter who took Samford's order doesn't even seem to notice his junk waving at her as the clone drags him outside.

"Where are you taking me?" Samford cries as the clone throws him on the curb. The concrete is warm against his bare ass.

"Shut your mouth, Sam," the clone shouts. "I'll do all the talking. You just listen." The clone lowers his voice. "Look, I need your help. You're the only one who can help me."

Samford is relieved by the sudden change of tone. "I'd be happy to help," Samford says. The clone offers a hand and pulls Samford to his feet. Then the clone reaches down and grabs Samford's pants. In one quick motion, he pulls them up to Samford's waist, covering his real genitals.

"So what exactly do you need?"

"I said no questions!" the clone yells before striking Samford in the face. The blow sends Samford through the glass pane of the Arby's front door.

"Get up, now!" the clone yells. He doesn't help Samford this time. "Stop being a pussy. I won't have my real be a pussy."

Samford slowly stands. He is frightened of the clone's power and temper. He wonders why *he* isn't that strong.

The clone grabs Samford and tosses him in the trunk of a white Ford. As the car speeds away from Arby's, Samford's body is flung around the spacious trunk. Still, Samford is glad to be riding in the dark and not up front with the ugly, menacing clone.

Roadies

by Kimberlee Smith

I don't know where my husband Dean is, and I'm not that interested in finding out right about now. I am transfixed. This is what I watch my mum Maybell pack up for our baby daughter Etheline and for herself: bottled water, canned sausages, two serrated knives, adult diapers size medium, lime cordial, several bottles of gin, a case of instant oatmeal and boxes of sultanas to go with it, cases of pureed baby food, peanut butter, wet wipes, kitchen-size plastic rubbish bags, her Ouija board, disposable baby nappies size six-to-nine months, plastic jugs filled with tap water, her favorite blanket, a fishing pole and lures she fixed from chook hackles, and the toy rattle Dean made for our daughter from dozens of real snake-tail rattles.

They're ready to roll and I know where they're going. If I could ask Mum one question at this moment, it would be, *Why did you wait so long?*

I don't remember the last time I was this excited. Like bouncing off the walls excited. She is heading out on a road trip to find her ex-husband, who also happens to be my daddy, who also happens to go by the name of Brother Tom Bend. He is a preacher. But not just any preacher.

He's also the founder of the Signs of Holiness Supreme Divinity Evangelical congregation. He and Mum traveled all around the continent spreading the word as soon as they were married. She was sixteen years old, and he was twenty-two.

They had me a year later and then of course I went with them. He took us with him on the evangelical gypsy caravan until one day we settled down so I could go to a proper school like regular kids. I was twelve, thirteen. Mum was good at schooling me at home, so I caught up all right. Then Brother Tom left. I've been waiting ever since to find out why. And Mum? She's been, well, mum. Never could get her to talk about them breaking up. Maybe on this trip I'll finally learn the real truth.

Brother Tom doesn't know he has a granddaughter. She's his first grandchild, and she's going to be his only. That's on account of me being his only child and that I died the same day my baby was born. She arrived in the living world by Caesarean section seconds before I arrived in this afterworld. It was a snakebite. Pardon. Snakebites. Multiple bites, one snake.

Brother Tom has some current events to catch up with; he has no cellular phone that we know of and the places he travels are generally so remote they're off the map. And to add to the alien nature of this whole situation, we haven't physically seen him since I was sixteen. Brother Tom told me I was old enough to take a husband of my own, so we were to take care of each other – and my mum – from then on.

Maybell – who is now Etheline's sole guardian – and Etheline are about to hit the road this arvo after tea. They're taking my old Jackaroo with bald tires and a petrol gauge that's perpetually stuck on one-third of a tank, no matter how much you fill it.

The snakes Dean left behind were well cared for and could be left alone for months. Mum slowly lowered the temperature in the room she relocated them to and dimmed the lights so they would naturally be inclined to hibernate. She fed them plenty of the mice Dean raised as food and then put the rest in brown cardboard boxes and let them loose in the bush. She locked up the house, and left the snakes behind. Can you imagine if the neighbors were to ever find out?

Etheline's bouncing every which way strapped into her car seat, sucking on the rattle Dean made for her, and having a good giggle now, but considering the driving trip to find Brother Tom will take weeks I reckon little Etheline's mood will turn in short order. Yet Maybell knows exactly what to do to soothe her.

Brother Tom is revered for his serpent handling, which is illegal here in Australia. All my life I saw him handle serpents and he was bitten probably a dozen times. Lost two fingers. Never once went to hospital. The bites just cured on their own.

Mum handled at least as many serpents as Brother Tom without being bitten. He believed she had been anointed by the Holy Spirit. She allowed him that. But she understood the serpents' nerves, and they picked up on it. Fell floppy as rag dolls in her hands.

What Mum's gleaned from members of the church is he's parked his caravan at Kununurra, in the Kimberley. It's an inhospitable place, where barramundi jump right out of the rivers and bite you in the ass and crocodiles drag you down under in the billabong and drown you before they tear you up for tea.

Kununurra is "God's country": unspoiled and virginal. The most pristine place on earth.

But Brother Tom's always had the passion to convert folks to his beliefs – it's in his head and in his heart and nobody can change the way that man operates. You'd figure he might want to find a way to save his family before taking on the rest of the world, but then again most people would rather take on the rest of the world than tackle their most intimate problems.

Mum's headed toward the Red Center. She's passed over the North Bourke Bridge and is heading toward the banks of the Darling. She's always wanted to see Uluru for real, and now she's going to have her wish come true, sleeping under the stars in the shadow of the rock, marveling at bands of wild camels, and eating skewered emu cooked on the barbie, all the while taking care of a baby and in the wake of having lost most of her family. For a woman who spent her adult life following her husband around, she sure does have a will of her own and an adventurous side. I never did know for sure she could do it alone. I'd rather she didn't have to, though. I wish I'd been able to share that with Mum while I was alive.

Now, Mum's been driving for about eight hours and finally is stopping. A place called Trilby Station that advertised "outback accommodations" on a roadside sign. There are caravan hookups and I bet this is the first time Mum will have missed the old caravan we lived in for so many years.

She's only stopped to refuel, give a bottle to the bub, and change her nappy. I wondered why Mum brought adult nappies but now I know too much. She hasn't had to stop to use the loo since she's been driving. Dear Lord. She's a woman on a mission, being maybe more passionate about this trip than Brother Tom could ever dream of being about his religious calling. And our sweet little bub, she knows her mum and daddy – albeit her highly distracted and fidgety daddy – are right here with her, looking down on her. I've tried to connect with Maybell as well, but with no

131

success. It seems as if something is blocking our connection.

I reckon by the time they reach their final destination, Etheline will have cut a couple teeth and be able to sit up all by herself. She will know how to clap her hands and play peek-a-boo. But she still will not know what it's like for her mum to hold her. I hope it's a very, very long time before she and I are reunited in my world.

Family Values

by Vanessa Weibler Paris

"Don't rely on others for your happiness," I start. "You're responsible for your own happiness."

"Never admit weakness," Iris says without missing a beat.

It's a game Iris invented. She comes up with a topic, and then we ping-pong back and forth until someone is stumped or gives up. Tonight's topic is "Family Values (Things My Family Taught Me Without Me Even Realizing It)."

"Don't vote Republican," I offer.

"Everything you do reflects on your parents," Iris responds.

"If it's worth doing, it's worth doing well," I counter.

"Emotions should be kept private," says Iris. Sitting at the kitchen island, she's licking blackstrap molasses off the serrated blade of a steak knife. She does it every morning. Blackstrap molasses, she tells me, is full of iron and calcium. Full of *strength*.

"If you're not five minutes early, you're late," from me.

"Don't stand out," says Iris. "Conform."

She dips into the jar and licks, dips and licks, running her tongue over sharp silver teeth as the molasses stretches slowly, thickly along its edge. I watch, as always, for a burst of blood, but there is none. "Doesn't it hurt?" I'd once asked. "Yes," she'd replied, nothing more.

I can think of more – *you are expected to attend college, what goes around comes around, you can succeed at anything you put your mind to* – but fold instead. Iris likes to win.

This woman, when she met me for our first date, looked like any other woman on an evening date: little black dress (standard, slimming), dramatic eye makeup (sexy, smoky), and crimson lips.

What I didn't know then was this: That wasn't Iris on a first date, that was just *Iris*. Even now, at my kitchen island, she's in full eye makeup, with a tight black top, jeans, and bare feet with black toenails.

It takes a while to get to know someone.

"I'm an artist," she'd shared that first night. Weeks later she opened a closet and showed me the pieces of her first exhibit. She'd collected dozens of x-rays of broken bones, then arranged them into a glowing new person. Completely whole, and entirely broken. A body that, if real, might collapse hollow and clattering into a pile of shards if poked hard. "The left hand was mine," she'd whispered close, another night, when we weren't talking at all. "I used a hammer. I screamed." My left hand, on her thigh, shook.

"I actually kind of like skinny guys," she'd mentioned that first night. Now she warns me not to eat too many wings when I go out with Bobby and the boys; she doesn't want me to put on weight. She stuffs my baggy clothes in the laundry and stocks the drawers with new ones, small ones that show just how thin I am. She asks me to pull up a sleeve or hoist up a pant leg so she can touch the bone beneath. "I wish I could hold it tight," she says, making a circle of her thumb and forefinger, wrapping them around my forearm or ankle, straining to touch their tips. "If it were just a little smaller ..."

We haven't had sex yet. She says it will be soon.

I hear a tiny gasp and turn around. Iris is looking at the knife, smeared with black and red, and blood stains her mouth like crimson lipstick.

"Kiss me," she says, and I do, pressing on her softness as she leans into my sharp.

"You taste bitter," I whisper. "But I like it."

"Because it is bitter," she responds, circling my wrists hard with both hands, "and because it is my heart."

Wednesday

30

July
2014

The Getaway

by Joanne Jagoda

It's 5:30. If I see those damn green numbers one more time I'm going to puke. Why doesn't the time go faster? I'm packed though it took me all night. I splurged on a few new outfits and that sexy one shoulder black bathing suit, but I'll regret it when the bills come. Oh hell, for once I don't care. David is picking me up at ten. I've got to keep busy until then. I'll pay bills, dust and water the plants.

I need strong coffee. The twins won't be up for another hour. They're going to their summer jobs and will be gone before David comes. It's better this way. Robin is still giving me a hard time about him. This pile of magazines keeps getting bigger, but I don't want to throw them out with the articles about their grandfather's company. It's been exciting. George has been interviewed on the news and written up in all kinds of newspapers and magazines. He'll even be on 60 Minutes next week. I didn't know he has been working on this top-secret project for years, a sophisticated rocket receptor system known as Project Octopus. Israel used a similar version, their Iron Dome, in the Gaza War in 2012. I read that the new system is more advanced as it intercepts medium to long-range rockets from a much further distance.

Lucky for us George is so successful. He's covering the girls' tuition. It's been rough since Paul died. Without

George and Lillian's help, I would've lost the house, and I don't know how I could have paid their college bills.

I'll put stamps on these bills and shower. I'll wear my new fuchsia cropped pants and a tight black tee-shirt. I only need to tussle my hair and add a sporty cap in case David has the top down. I hope he does even if it's cold. Lucky he was able to get away mid-week. I didn't want to be gone from the girls on the weekend.

"You look cute Mom. Have fun and be good."

"Thanks Cassie. Grab my suitcase and bring it downstairs."

"Uhhh … what **do** you have in here? Rob, Mom's going for two months. What's for lunch Rob?"

"I made you a peanut butter sandwich. Mom, I don't like him. You can cancel. Say you're sick. Say you came down with a rare disease that's catchy. Come on Cass. I'll drop you at BART."

"Oh Rob, I just don't get your attitude … And don't SLAM the door."

Why is she so against David? She can be so unreasonable. I love this picture of the four of us in Maui. Oh Paul, I miss those fun times when life was simpler.

* * * * *

Nobody on the street, just that utility truck again. I feel like I'm being watched. I'm usually the "watcher." I'm going to get to my car from the basement. There's a back door to the street. Good I left my car four blocks away in an alley. Those assholes don't trust me. If this operation I've been working on for months isn't successful, they'll go after me. I'll be fish food in San Francisco Bay. When I found out yesterday the final testing won't be complete for a month, I had to cancel my plans for the kidnap to happen today *while we're in the Napa Valley. My employers were not happy. I explained to them that I have to keep cozying up to Anne for this all to work and things can't be rushed, but they don't get it.*

I'm glad I ditched that shitty rental for this BMW convertible. This charade is getting to be a chore though I suppose sleeping with Anne today won't be a bad perk of this assignment. Once this assignment is complete, I'll leave for South America and disappear. With my flawless Spanish, I'll blend in easily and have plenty of money to enjoy. Hopefully Grandpa George will give up the specs promptly. I won't relish hurting Cassie, though I'll do what I need to do.

Ah Anne, in another life I could have loved a sweet thing like you. Oh, she's opening the door before I can even ring. She's waiting for me. Sweet foolish girl.

"Hi David. I like your sporty cargo shorts and Giants cap."

"Hi darlin', and you look adorable. Give me your suitcase. Whoa, you didn't tell me we're going for a month."

"Very funny. I wasn't sure what to bring so I brought everything."

"Want to hear the lads from Liverpool?"

"I love the Beatles."

"You know all the words but you're way off key. Here we are at the Sattui winery. First we'll taste some of the Sattui wines. I'll get us a bottle of whichever you like and we'll picnic on their grounds."

"I like their merlot the best."

"Good choice Annie. Their 2011 Napa Valley Merlot is outstanding. Ready for lunch?"

"My tummy is growling. While you pay for the wine, I'll get in the deli line. So much to choose from. Mmmm, the roast turkey looks good, some cheeses, that broccoli raisin salad and a long baguette."

"And I'll find us a picnic table in the shade."

"This spot is perfect. I love looking out at the vineyards. It feels like we are in France, instead of an hour and a half from San Francisco. Mmmm, taste the broccoli salad. It's so good and this brie is ..."

I know I'm being watched. Maybe it is the two men at the table over to the right who look like rednecks with big beer bellies or that olive-skinned man to the left in the '49er cap. Got to get away from here. It's too exposed. My employers obviously don't trust me or maybe somebody else wants the plans to Project Octopus.

"Let's go, Ann."

"David, why rush? I'm still eating."

"No, got to go NOW. We have spa appointments. Finish eating in the car."

I'm checking the mirror. Good thing Anne is oblivious. She's absorbed in the beautiful scenery of Highway 29, the oak trees lining the road and the acres of vineyards. Can't blame her for that. Seventeen miles to Calistoga. I booked mud baths at a fancy spa. Nice to spend money that's not mine.

"Never had a mud bath. I'm glad we're next to each other. Ohhh, it's squishy. Very warm."

"You're in volcanic ash. Great healing powers." *It's even making me relax. Maybe I'm just being paranoid about someone following me but I'm a pro at this business.*

"It's so fun to be in tubs next to each other. Then massages. I feel like a pampered princess."

§

"David, this hotel room is elegant. I'll be back in a minute."

"Annie, I thought you were tired. Very nice, your lacy black nightgown."

"It's been a long while David. I've been uh … looking forward to being with you."

She's an awesome lover. I'm such a shit to use her. "Let's get ready for dinner. I have reservations at Bouchon, a world class restaurant, Michelin rated."

"That sounds fantastic. I'll just shower, but first I want to check on the girls."

"Hi Cassie, how was work?"

"Fine. Having fun Mom?"

"I had a mud bath and massage. We're going to a fancy restaurant. I feel like a princess. Can I speak to your sister?"

"Uh, well she's not here."

"She was supposed to come home from work and stay at Denise's with you. Where is she?"

"Mom, I promised I wouldn't tell."

"Cassie, I'm not amused."

"She went over to Patty's house. They're going to a rave in the Mission later tonight."

"A **what**?"

"A rave. She'll kill me."

"Now I'm pissed."

"Let me try to call her Mom."

"Anne, you're going to wear a hole in the carpet. Relax, she's fine." *Robin's a little shit.*

"David, I have a right to be worried. She's just … There's my phone!"

"Cass, did you reach her?"

"Mom, it's Rob. Can you chill? I'm not going to the rave. I figured out it was a crappy thing to do. You have to

140

give me a little space. We're all going to a late movie. Heard you had a mud bath. Oooh yuck."

"Thanks Robin. Love you honey and uh ... glad you checked in."

"David, come here. You were right. I shouldn't worry so much."

"Mmmm, Annie, I do like your kisses. No more fretting over Robin. We better hurry or we'll be late for our reservation although ... mmm, yes, you do have the nicest bum and perfect breasts. While you're showering I'll be outside by the pools."

I thought I saw that olive-skinned man on a lawn chair by the pool. Is that him in the deep end?

Thursday

31

July
2014

Hijinks Ensue

by h. l. nelson

Dear Diary,

Oh my god, I'm dying, this is so hilarious. I just returned from a StrollerFit class, where Robin, Julie, and I wrapped dolls up in baby blankets and put them in our strollers, then we pretended to trip and dump our "babies" on the ground, pull up our shirts to "breastfeed" without covering up, and be obnoxious and competitive "new moms" about our babies' height, weight, and head measurements. The other women caught on after about twenty minutes and insisted we leave. But, it sure was a riot! We collapsed in my car, crying from laughter. It was one of the best things we've pulled off in the last two months.

Let me back up, though, because you, dear diary, have no idea how the hell this all began. I shall enlighten you, then I must be off to my painting class at 2 P.M.

As soon as school let out in early June and we all found ways to busy our children, like summer camps, jobs, and visits to relatives, Julie, Robin and I started meeting at my house. Robin and Anne had had a falling out for the hundredth time, this time because Anne swore Robin stole liquor from Anne's cabinet. And Julie, of course, just followed along. I'm pretty sure she dislikes pampered Anne and her bleached butthole as much as we do, but she's just quiet about it. Anyway, Robin later told me that she had actually taken the alcohol, which I thought was hysterical. My hatred for Anne has blossomed over this latest installment of 'Anne's Winter Wonderland'. This year, she seems hell-bent on making us all her personal slaves. I told Anne to stick the party, all the hors d'oeuvres, the goddamn ice sculptures, the Alpine mountain of Swiss chocolate she's having flown in, up her perfectly bleached asshole.

So the three of us had my house to ourselves all day, and I had decided that we needed to start our own Moms' Revolution. When I said the words "Moms' Revolution," a slow Cheshire-cat grin spread across Robin's face and Julie's eyes bugged so big I thought they would pop out of her head. Exactly the response I thought I'd get. For a week, I'd been staying up late in my art room and planning out our revolution.

One night, Brandon had come in behind me without me hearing. I don't know how long he'd been standing there, but he said, "What do 'Perfume to Piss', 'Mutilated Machines', and 'StrollerShit' mean? I slammed my laptop down and said, "Why in the hell did you sneak up on me like that?"

He folded his arms. "Look, Joan, I don't care what kind of weird stuff you're writing or whatever, we just haven't talked much for a while and I thought I'd see if you wanted to spend some time together. I guess not." Then he left before I could answer him. The truth was, I barely thought about him anymore. He spent most nights at work, so the kids and I had learned to get on without him. This made me feel sad. Years we'd spent tied at the hip – trying weird restaurants like the Pho Florence, the Thai / Italian place that was open for four months; making love in crazy places like the exit hallways of malls; curling up together every evening on the couch. When did we stop doing these things? After the kids were born, of course. I totally understand why people get divorced more often after having kids – they're super stressful.

143

Anyway, I decided I would make up with him later. The work I was about to do with the ladies was important.

So, to loosen us up, Project Mutilated Machines was first up. That was about a month ago. It had already started to get hot outside. We piled all of Robin's kitchen appliances on her back veranda. Robin had brought one of her own, the dreaded Foreman grill. It was awkward, seeing all that metal and plastic splayed out in the afternoon sun. Like prostitutes at a barn raising. For a minute, we didn't know what to do. They both looked at me. Then, I said, "Fuck it" and swung the Louisville Slugger down onto the juicer. Jagged bits of plastic flew in all directions. Julie covered her eyes and Robin war-whooped. I must say, it felt good. It felt damn good.

By the end of it, we were screaming at the top of our lungs as we pummeled the sad machinery. Julie yelled, "No, I don't want to host another dinner party for your boss who loves burgers! I fucking HATE – GEORGE – FOREMAN!" punctuating each word with a smash of her bat into the small black appliance. Robin, green-kneed, was punishing pieces of her bread maker that had attempted escape onto the lawn. Her ponytail had fallen and she looked crazed with her bugged eyes and spittle on her bottom lip. It was like Nazi Germany all over again, right here in Palm Valley. But the Jews were made of plastic and metal.

Afterward, we surveyed the destruction, smoothing our hair and re-tucking our blouses. We felt a new respect for each other. I could see it in their eyes. And for ourselves. There was no going back.

A week later, we walked into the mall like it was a normal day, just three women shopping together. Stopping at the food court, we ordered Cinnabun rolls and ate them standing up, the sugar making our lips stick together. I hadn't eaten sweets with such abandon since I was a kid.

144

We yelled at passing teens and 20-something boys, hooted and hollered, "Hey, you want some of this?" A security officer peered at us, but didn't do anything. What was he going to do? Forever 21 was having a sale on thongs, so after sugaring up, we sauntered in and asked the checker to go to the back and look for items we each wanted. Like a fur-lined velvet zipper vest in size 4, for me, a red sequined scoop-necked halter top in size 6 for Robin, and a champagne-colored velour jumpsuit in size 2 for Julie. I told her we'd tried on all of these pieces the weekend before, so they simply had to have them in stock.

When she'd gone in the back after some convincing with a fifty dollar bill, a perplexed look on her face, we dug into the huge bin full of thongs and stretching them out between our fingers, we shot them across the store at each other until the checker returned. Well, Robin and I shot them at each other and Julie. Surprisingly, the checker came out from the back with almost exactly what we'd asked for. That gave us a good laugh. Even though none of the sizes fit us, of course, I paid for the items to immortalize the day.

At The Gap, Robin and I pretended to be mannequins, except Mannequin Robin tweaked Mannequin Me's tits, as I stuck them out proudly. Several teens stopped, laughed, and snapped pictures.

Hanging around until near closing time, we finally headed to Macy's. Kendra let us in, a big smile on her face. Brandon and I had made her and Kurt get jobs last month so they can really understand what it means to work. She hates that job, and I don't blame her. I remember working retail, too. She whispered that she had cut the feed to the security camera in the beauty department, said it would look like it was a technical glitch. Perfect. And no, I don't feel guilty at all about having had Kendra help. She has to learn that this "beauty" industry is a load of fucking bullshit. Buy this cream, primp that, lose the fat. She's started to look at me differently, act more respectfully. She and Kurt, both. It's been good for my relationships with them, overall. This makes me happy.

What we did was we dumped all of the Dolce and Gabbana, Juicy Couture, CK perfumes into a plastic container, leaving a little in the bottom of each bottle. Whew, it smelled like all the chicks from a whorehouse and a strip club got together in the same room. Then, using a funnel, we filled up the perfume bottles with our piss. We'd each been collecting it for a week. Even Julie thought this prank was funny, but she's allergic to most perfumes. Man, I wish I could see the faces of the women who buy our eau de toilet.

I have to pick up the kids from their jobs soon – Kurt from Scoops ice cream and Kendra from Macy's, but it's been real, dear diary. I'm going to take them to the beach for being such awesome kids lately.

Love,

Joan StrollerFit-Champ-Beat-Your-Appliances-and-Urinate-In-The-Beauty-Industry's-Bottle Colderman

Authors

Rachel Ambrose is a twenty-something fiction writer from Connecticut. Her favorite season is winter, she enjoys well-made Manhattans, and she loves Southern fiction. Her work has appeared in *Crack the Spine*, *Exiles Literary Magazine*, and *The Colton Review*. Currently at work on her second novel, she blogs at http://victorywhiskeyjuliet.tumblr.com.

Lynn Beighley is a fiction writer stuck in a technical book writer's body. Her stories often involve deeply flawed characters and the unsatisfying meshing of the virtual and actual world. She has an MFA in Creative Writing and currently has 16 books published.

Margaret Bingel is just a writer, living in Manchester, New Hampshire. She spends her time working at her father's beer store, art modeling, and writing (when she can). She doesn't have a website or a blog yet, but who knows, maybe she'll have one in the future.

Guilie Castillo-Oriard is a Mexican writer currently exiled in the island of Curaçao. She misses Mexican food and Mexican *amabilidad*, but the laissez-faire attitude and the beaches of the Caribbean are fair exchange. Plus, the bounty of cultural diversity inspires great culture-clash fiction. Guilie is currently revising and editing her first novel. Her short stories have appeared in *Fiction 365*, *Lady Ink Magazine* and *Pure Slush*. She blogs at http://guilie-castillo-oriard.blogspot.com.

John Wentworth Chapin lives and writes in Baltimore, where he is too frequently starting Project B before finishing Project A. John writes non-fiction as well as fiction. Find him on the web at http://johnwentworthchapin.com.

James Claffey hails from County Westmeath, Ireland, and lives on an avocado ranch in Carpinteria, CA with his family. He is the author of a collection of short fiction, *Blood a Cold Blue*. His website can be found at http://jamesclaffey.com.

Gay Degani has published online and in print including *The Best of Every Day Fiction* editions and her own collection, *Pomegranate Stories*. She is the founder-editor emeritus of EDF's *Flash Fiction Chronicles*, a staff editor at *Smokelong Quarterly*, and blogs at *Words in Place* where a list of her work can be found. She's had two stories nominated for Pushcart consideration and won the eleventh Annual Glass Woman Prize for her flash piece, *Something about L.A.*

Michelle Elvy is an editor and writer who has meandered from the shores of the Chesapeake to New Zealand's Bay of Islands. Michelle has published poetry, short stories and non-fiction about travel, faraway places, food, motorcycling, slow travel, the kindness of strangers and raising children in unusual places for numerous literary journals and magazines in the US, Canada, Australasia, UK and Europe. She edits at *Flash Frontier: An Adventure in Short Fiction* and *Blue Five Notebook*. She can also be found regularly at *Awkword Paper Cut*. More about manuscript assessment and Michelle's take on editing and writing at http://michelleelvy.com.

Gloria Garfunkel is the daughter of two Auschwitz survivors which deeply affected her whole life and personality. She has a Ph.D. from Harvard University in Psychology and Social Relations, concentrating on Personality Development Studies. She was a psychotherapist for thirty years working with children, adults and families. She is currently retired, reading and writing to her heart's content. She has published many stories in journals and anthologies and hopes to eventually publish a collection of her flash fiction. Find more at her blog http://queruloussquirreldaily.blogspot.com/

Teresa Burns Gunther has had fiction and non-fiction appear in numerous literary journals and most recently in *Northwind Magazine*, *Bookslut* and *Best New Writing 2012*. Teresa is the Editor of *The Lakeside*, an online literary magazine, and she founded Lakeshore Writers Workshop in Oakland, California where she leads creative writing workshops and classes and works one-on-one with writers. Find her work at http://www.teresaburnsgunther.com/.

Gill Hoffs lives with her family and an ever-dwindling supply of Nutella in the North of England. Find Gill on facebook or as @gillhoffs on twitter, email her a dirty joke at gillhoffs@hotmail.co.uk, or leave a clean comment at http://gillhoffs.wordpress.com/. *Wild: a collection* is out now from *Pure Slush Books*. Her non-fiction book *The Sinking of RMS Tayleur: the Lost Story of the Victorian Titanic* is also out now, from Pen & Sword. (See her site or http://www.pen-and-sword.co.uk/ for details.) Feel free to send her chocolate.

Joanne Jagoda of Oakland, California, took an inspiring writing workshop after retiring in 2009, and launched on a long-postponed creative writing journey. Since discovering her passion for writing, she has worked non-stop on short stories, poetry and non-fiction. Her work has appeared in a number of e-zines and print anthologies, including *Pure Slush* and *Idea Gems Magazine*, and she was a poet of the month for a Jewish news weekly in Northern California. When not taking writing and poetry classes, Joanne enjoys being a writer-coach for ninth graders, Zumba, and visiting her three grandchildren in Jerusalem.

Len Kuntz is a writer from Washington State and an editor at the online literary magazine Metazen. His work appears widely in print and online. You can find more of his work at http://lenkuntz.blogspot.com.

Sally-Anne Macomber was born and raised in Toronto, Canada, and studied journalism at Concordia University in Montreal. Her work on high fashion and the demise of haute couture has appeared in various online and print publications in both Europe and North America. She turned to writing flash fiction in 2010, and hasn't looked back.

Jessica McHugh is an author of speculative fiction that spans the genre from horror and alternate history to epic fantasy. A member of the Horror Writers Association and a 2013 Pulp Ark nominee, she has devoted herself to novels, short stories, poetry, and playwriting. Jessica has had thirteen books published in five years, including the bestselling *Rabbits in the Garden*, *The Sky: The World* and the gritty coming-of-age thriller, *PINS*. More info on her speculations and publications can be found at http://www.jessicamchughbooks.com.

Gwendolyn Joyce Mintz is a fiction writer and aspiring photographer. Her work has appeared in various online and print publications. In other incarnations, Mintz is a writing instructor, a teddy bear maker and somebody's grand-mother.

h. l. nelson is Founding Editor/Executive Director of *Cease, Cows* lit mag and a former sidewalk mannequin. Pub credits: *PANK, Hobart, Connotation Press, Metazen, Drunk Monkeys, Red Fez, Bartleby Snopes*. She's also editing an anthology which includes stories by Aimee Bender, Roxane Gay, Lindsay Hunter and other fierce women writers. Her MFA is currently kicking her ass. Tell her what you're wearing: heather@hlnelson.com.

Mandy Nicol grew up in Melbourne, Australia and made a tree change to country Victoria in the mid-nineties – the decade, not her age. She has various animals including a flockette of pet sheep that are thankful for her vegaquarian habits. She writes short stories and loves flash fiction. *Pure Slush* is the first venue to publish her work.

Derek Osborne lives in eastern Pennsylvania. His work has appeared in *Boston Literary Magazine, Bartleby Snopes, Literary Orphans, The Linnet's Wings, Pure Slush* and many others. To read more visit http://gertrudesflat.blogspot.com, or email him at derekosborne1@gmail.com.

Vanessa Weibler Paris lives in Erie, Pa., with a guy, a girl, a boy, a bunny rabbit and a dog. She writes things both real (for work) and pretend (for fun). Her favorite things include hot peppers, bad puns, small-world stories, and tales with a twist at the end.

Gary Percesepe is Associate Editor at *New World Writing* (formerly *Mississippi Review*) and a Contributor at *The*

Nervous Breakdown. Author of four books in philosophy, Percesepe's poetry, fiction, essays, and interviews have appeared in *Story Quarterly*, *N + 1*, *Salon*, *Mississippi Review*, *The Millions*, *Brevity*, *PANK*, *Metazen*, *The Brooklyner*, and other places. His collection of short stories, *Why I Did the Grocery Girl*, is forthcoming from Aqueous Books. His poetry collection *falling* and his flash fiction collection *itch* were published by *Pure Slush Books* in late 2013. He has taught at Saint Louis University, Wittenberg University, and University of Dayton. He lives in Buffalo, New York.

Matt Potter is an Australian-born writer who keeps a part of his psyche in Berlin. Matt has been published in various places online, and he is, rather amazingly, also the founding editor of *Pure Slush*. You can find more of his work at his website: http://mattcpotter.webs.com/.

Darryl Price was born in Kentucky and educated at Thomas More College. A founding member of L. Jack Roth's Yellow Pages Poets, he has published dozens of chapbooks, and his poems have appeared in many journals. He currently edits *Olentangy Review* with his wife Melissa.

Stephen V. Ramey is an American author from New Castle, Pennsylvania. His work has appeared in many places, including *The Doctor TJ Eckleburg Review*, *The Journal of Compressed Creative Arts*, and *A Capella Zoo*. *Glass Animals*, his first collection of (very) short fiction is available from *Pure Slush Books*. Find him and more of his work at http://www.stephenvramey.com.

Shane Simmons is a self-confessed coffee shop writer who believes that regardless of quality, each paragraph penned should be rewarded with sweet treats (cake, muffins, Belgian waffles, etc). London-born, he ran away to Glasgow ten years ago, expanded his waistline and now blogs at http://scribblingsimmons.wordpress.com/.

Kimberlee Smith is a writer whose poetry, essays, fiction, and creative non-fiction have been published in numerous literary journals and anthologies. She was awarded a residency to the Jentel Arts Program in 2013. She lives with her two daughters, two dogs, three cats, two rabbits, and nine chooks on her farm in rural Connecticut. She received her MA in English from the University of Sydney, a certificate in the Creative Writing Program through UCLA, and her BA in Journalism from the University of Southern California. She is enrolled currently in post-graduate studies at Columbia University in New York. She can do a headstand on a trampoline, kill a chook, and make hard cider from the apples in her orchard.

Andrew Stancek was born in Bratislava and saw Russian tanks occupying his homeland. His dreams of circuses and ice cream, flying and lion-taming, miracle and romance have appeared recently in print in *LA Review, Windsor Review* and *New Sun Rising: Stories for Japan*. Among the many online publications featuring his work are *Every Day Fiction, Gemini Magazine* (Flash Fiction Contest Grand Prize Winner), *fwriction, r.kv.r.y. quarterly literary journal, Tin House, Flash Fiction* Chronicles, *The Linnet's Wings, Connotation Press, THIS Literary Magazine, LA Review, Windsor Review, Thrice Fiction Magazine, New Sun Rising,* and *Pure Slush* online.

Susan Tepper is the author of four published books of fiction and a chapbook of poetry. Her most recent title *The Merrill Diaries* (*Pure Slush Books,* July 2013) is a Novel in Stories that follow a young woman's adventures in love and lust on two continents, spanning a decade. Tepper has received nine Pushcart nominations, and one for the

Pulitzer Prize in fiction. You can visit her website here: http://www.susantepper.com.

Nathaniel Tower lives in the Twin Cities with his wife and daughter. After teaching high school English for nine years, he decided to pursue a career in writing / publishing / editing. His fiction has appeared in over two hundred online and print journals. His first collection of fiction, *Nagging Wives, Foolish Husbands*, was released in 2014 through *Martian Lit*. Nathaniel is the founding and managing editor of *Bartleby Snopes Literary Magazine and Press*. You can find out more about Nathaniel at http://nathanieltower.wordpress.com.

Townsend Walker lives in San Francisco. His stories have been published in over fifty literary journals and included in seven anthologies. One story won the SLO NightWriters story contest. Two were nominated for the PEN / O. Henry Award. Four were performed at the New Short Fiction Series in Hollywood. He is associate editor at *Grey Sparrow Journal*. During a career in finance he published three books, on foreign exchange, derivatives and portfolio management. Educated at Georgetown, NYU and Stanford, his website is at http://www.townsendwalker.com.

Michael Webb is continually surprised anyone is interested in what he has to say, and he blogs occasionally at http://innocentsaccidentshints.blogspot.com.

Other volumes in the *2014* series from Pure Slush

Visit the Pure Slush Store:
http://pureslush.webs.com/store.htm

April 2014 Vol. 4
ISBN: 978-1-925101-27-0

May 2014 Vol. 5
ISBN: 978-1-925101-30-0

June 2014 Vol. 6
ISBN: 978-1-925101-49-2

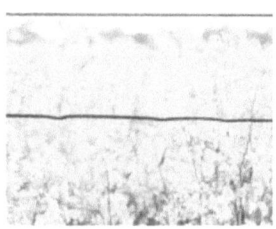

August 2014 Vol. 8
ISBN: 978-1-925101-40-9

September 2014 Vol. 9
ISBN: 978-1-925101-43-0

October 2014 Vol. 10
ISBN: 978-1-925101-50-8